"Hang on!" Cade ye

The cruiser struck the soft ground and bounced wildly. Cade hit the retro jets, feeling the cruiser shudder and yaw to the right. Losing its flight ability, the aircraft became a dead weight. It careered violently, slithering in a wide arc, and came to an abrupt stop against a tree. The canopy shattered, showering Cade and Janek with Plexiglas as they were thrown forward against the seat restraints.

Janek twisted around as he picked up the noise of the combat chopper. A shadow began to slide across the ground, converging on the downed cruiser. "Time to move on," he said, thumping the emergency hatch release.

They cleared the cruiser seconds before a raking blast from the chopper's cannon tore through the passenger compartment. The heat blast from the exploding fuel tank singed their clothing as they hit the ground, scrambling for safety. Flaming fuel rained down around them, blown by the rotor wash from the settling chopper.

Cade pulled his autopistol, peering through the swirl of smoke. He watched the three-man team jump from the helicopter, their combat rifles at the ready as they began to fan out.

CADE

MIKE LINAKER

Hardcase

A GOLD EAGLE BOOK FROM

WORLDWIDE®

TORONTO • NEW YORK • LONDON
AMSTERDAM • PARIS • SYDNEY • HAMBURG
STOCKHOLM • ATHENS • TOKYO • MILAN
MADRID • WARSAW • BUDAPEST • AUCKLAND

First edition September 1992

ISBN 0-373-63805-1

HARDCASE

PROLOGUE

George Takagi's life ended the moment he walked out of the NYPD headquarters building. He didn't realize he was a dead man at the time, so he continued on to the parking lot and climbed into his car. He was anxious to make the rendezvous he'd arranged some time earlier.

The meet was with an old friend. The one man in New York Takagi knew he could trust.

Thomas Jefferson Cade.

Cade the cop and Takagi the NYPD tech had known each other for a number of years prior to Cade's becoming a Justice marshal. They still kept in touch, meeting when Cade had to call in at the NYPD building on official business. Every so often they would get together over a beer, maybe a meal.

Tonight's meeting was far from social. It was strictly to do with police business, but it was the kind that Takagi believed had to be discussed off the record.

As a computer technician, Takagi was also responsible for evaluating data. His powerful computer banks enabled the Japanese-American to probe deep into information banks nationwide, as well as local. In his own right Takagi was a computer genius. He could almost make his machines stand up and salute the flag. When he'd been well into a search-and-evaluation program, from which he would be able to pinpoint increases or decreases in particular instances, Takagi's computer had locked in on a number of coroners' reports on sudden, violent deaths. That in itself was nothing outstanding.

Death was no novelty in 2055, and Takagi would have passed over the reports except for one thing.

The three deaths had all occurred within a two-day period, and the cause of death had been the same in each instance.

Someone had made an attempt to bury the reports in a limbo file, pushing them into an obscure corner of the New York Station Information Data Base. What they had omitted to do was to secure them with a strong enough restriction code. Takagi's computer, with its powerful search-and-retrieve program—devised by Takagi himself—had broken the code and thrown the reports up on his monitor. The program had simply been searching for information at Takagi's request.

Takagi, a mug of hot coffee in his hand, had sat staring at the screen text. He had read the reports over a number of times, silently asking the question, Why would anyone want to hide death reports?

Because there's something illegal going on, his police-trained mind had told him.

He'd paid closer attention to the text, reading the reports line for line. That was when he'd found the identical cause of death, which in itself was not unheard of, but this time the cause was unusual enough to make him look even harder.

Takagi had punched in to the National Computer Bank and requested a rundown on the three dead people—two men and one woman. Within a couple of minutes he had established a connection between them.

At the time of their deaths each of them had been employed by the Amosin Corporation.

Takagi knew of Amosin. It was a company with vast holdings. Amosin manufactured a wide range of electronic equipment, from computers to television sets to military hardware. Amosin Robotics were into domestic and combat droids. The company also owned and operated television channels, including the production and distribution of its own programs.

Takagi had started to get suspicious.

Three dead people.

Each had died in exactly the same way.

They had all worked for the same company.

And their deaths had been buried within the information system.

Too many coincidences.

Takagi had turned to his internal vid-phone, checking the indicator pad, and had seen that Captain Barney Culver, his boss, was still in his office. He'd reached across to punch in Culver's extension. Halfway through the exercise Takagi had stopped. He'd cancelled the number, leaning back in the comfortable swivel chair, his gaze drawn back to the monitor.

Deep inside something was telling him to cover his back. Before he showed his findings to anyone, he needed to take out some insurance.

Takagi couldn't have explained why the thought had occurred to him. Maybe it had been pure cop instinct taking over, his training coming through all the crap floating around inside his skull. Whatever it had been, Takagi had acted on it.

He'd reached for the vid-phone and punched through an outside number. While he'd waited for it to connect, he keyed in the command to connect the phone modem.

His call had connected and told him his party was out but he could leave a message if he wanted to. Takagi had.

He'd faced the vid-phone and explained what he'd found, his mounting suspicions and what he intended doing. Then he'd keyed in the command to have the computer relay the information it contained in its memory.

With that completed, Takagi had broken the connection and got through to Culver.

"You still here, George?" Culver's friendly voice had come over the line as his craggy, handsome face had swum into focus on the screen. "You okay?"

"Captain, I've got something I want to show you," Takagi had said. "Take a look at your monitor. I'm going to key some info through."

Culver had remained silent after Takagi had transferred the details. He was so quiet that Takagi had imagined he'd gone to sleep. After a few minutes Culver had swung back to face the screen.

"So?" he'd asked.

"Don't you think it's too much of a coincidence? Three dead. Time of death close together. Killed in the same way. And all working for Amosin. What do you think?"

"I think it's time you went home, George," Culver had said.

"Hey, I'm serious, Barney," Takagi had protested.

Culver had grinned. "So am I, buddy. I *know* how many hours you've put in today. All I want is for you to go home and get some rest. We'll get together tomorrow and sort this thing out."

Takagi had held the cop's steady gaze. He'd tried to make sense of Culver's reaction but failed. The only truth filtering through his brain had been the fact that he did feel bushed. Maybe it was time to call it a day.

"You still with me, George?"

"Yeah."

"So what do you say? Let me lock this stuff down. Hold it till morning so we can dig deeper."

Even then Takagi had resisted, and it must have shown on his face.

"Okay, George, time's up. Now I'm making it official. An order. You're off duty. Now get out of here and go home."

Culver had swung away from the vid-phone. Just before he'd broken the connection, Takagi had heard his final words.

"G'night, George."

The screen had flashed, then went blank.

Takagi had sat and stared at it.

His attention had been caught by movement on his computer's monitor. Swiveling around to face it, Takagi had seen the command display showing an intercept from an internal computer. Someone was transferring his data. He'd picked up on the input and recognized the transfer code as Culver's. The captain was accessing Takagi's files and pulling them out.

Takagi hadn't liked what he'd seen, but Culver's rank outclassed his own. He could access any department computer and take whatever information he wanted, no questions asked. Despite that, Takagi had felt there was something odd the way Culver was getting his hands on the information so fast. The tech had recalled the silence that had gripped Culver as he'd read the information. Thinking back, it had struck Takagi that maybe Culver hadn't expected to see such information on a monitor.

A strange unease had begun to grip him. He'd found he was experiencing traces of fear, and he hadn't felt secure in his own office any longer.

Something wasn't quite right.

It had to do with the death reports he'd unearthed... and Captain Barney Culver was involved. Takagi was certain of that now.

He'd decided the best thing he could do was get out of the office. In fact, out of the building.

He'd reached for his jacket and pulled it on. He'd turned to go, but hesitated, then crossed to the vidphone. He'd punched an outside line, then keyed in an autonumber. While he'd waited for the number to connect, Takagi had begun to sweat.

The call had been answered on the second tone. Takagi had almost yelled in relief when he'd recognized the face staring at him from the screen.

"Hello, George. Been a while."

"Listen, T.J., and do what I ask," Takagi had said.

"Okay," Cade had replied.

"I need to talk. Now. Soon as you can meet me."

Cade, sensing the urgency in Takagi's voice, had nodded.

"The old meeting place. Remember?"

"Sure, George. Hey—what's wrong?"

"I pulled some odd info out of the data bank. Tell you when I see you. Meet me in an hour."

Takagi had broken the connection, replacing the receiver as he'd turned for the door.

If he hadn't been in so much of a hurry, he might have picked up the faint electronic signal on the line as someone had listened in on a phone tap.

After he'd left his office, Takagi had taken an elevator to the basement garage. There he'd gone straight for his Ford 4x4 truck. Now behind the wheel, Takagi fired the engine and rolled out of the basement garage.

Leaving the NYPD building behind him, Takagi pushed into the heavy traffic and made his slow way across town until he was able to get onto Broadway. He sat in the lines of crawling vehicles, cursing New York's choked roads, the inadequate system that got worse with every passing year and the administration that failed to get a grip on the nightmare situation.

Although the city had always suffered from hot, humid spells, in recent decades this trend had intensified. The night was sullen with heat. For the past week the city had been sweltering beneath a harsh, cloudless blue sky. There was no breeze to relieve the monotonous oppression of the heat. The changed climate was another legacy of the environmental decay caused by ecological recklessness and the chemical attacks during the war that had lasted from 2034 to 2036.

The city might have been crumbling around the edges, services regularly breaking down and a crime rate soaring, but the relentless commercial hype went on. Takagi had plenty of time to read the advertisements blinking at him from every available space. Huge television screens, floating ad-drones, holographic displays. They flickered and cajoled the consumers day and night. Buy new cars. The latest domestic equipment. Housedroids. Vacations in space. Watch the new season's hit TV shows.

It never stopped. Never slackened. The messages intruded into daily life at a frenetic pace.

Takagi reached the meeting place ten minutes ahead of schedule, easing off Broadway, past the U.S. customs house, now a crumbling, semipreserved relic, and onto State Street. Traffic here was nil as Takagi slowed the 4x4, turning it across the green sward of Battery

Park. He parked and cut the power, sitting back and listening to the crack and ping of the 4x4's motor.

Beyond the Castle Clinton Monument, now housed in a plasdome where holographic historical displays entertained the tourists, Takagi caught a glimpse of the Hudson River's wide span. Feeling restless, Takagi climbed out of the stuffy cab, hoping to catch a trace of cool air from the river. He leaned against the door.

He felt the faint breeze first, the warm air drifting by his face. It took a few moments for him to realize he wasn't feeling natural air movement. It was pushing down from above, accompanied by a soft, almost inaudible whooshing sound. . . .

Curious, Takagi stepped away from the side of the 4x4, glancing skyward.

He saw it descending toward him. A sleek, dark shape swooping down out of the night sky on near-silent rotors.

It was a Skorpion-2 combat helicopter. A fast, deadly and heavily armed assault craft. As far as Takagi knew, they were only available for military use.

The chopper angled in toward the ground, barely making a sound. Matt black, with a dark Plexiglas canopy, it resembled a darting insect.

As the Skorpion hovered close by, Takagi saw dark figures drop from open hatches, then spread out after they hit the ground. As soon as the chopper had offloaded its passengers, it climbed rapidly, sweeping off across the park.

Takagi reached under his jacket for the NYPD standard-issue autopistol holstered on his belt. He had managed to clear leather and slip off the safety before the advancing figures from the choppers passed through a patch of moonlight.

Takagi recognized them instantly.

Dull black in color. Powerful humanoid shapes encased in titanium armor casings. Skull-like heads with taut, angular features that emphasized their hostile attitude.

Combat droids, designed and built for a single purpose—killing.

The droids were a military-only piece of hardware. So what were they doing in New York?

Takagi knew the answer.

They were after him.

He reacted instinctively. Even though he'd been off the streets for more than three years, he was still driven by the gut instinct of a street cop, and he responded to the threat. Ducking low, he rolled beneath the 4x4, wriggling to the far side of the vehicle. A gasp of pain burst from his lips as he came up against the hot exhaust pipe. He scrambled clear of the truck and shoved himself to his feet.

A droid lunged into view from the truck's rear, and its stubby submachine gun began to track in on Takagi.

The tech fired first, punching a trio of slugs at the combat droid. The high-velocity projectiles simply bounced off the matt black body armor.

"Hell!" Takagi muttered. In his haste he'd forgotten the single most important rule when dealing with droids. Always go for the eyes. The weakest point.

He flipped up the autopistol's muzzle for another shot.

This time the droid fired first. A stream of hollow-point slugs burned into Takagi's chest. The slugs expanded on impact, tearing through tissue and muscle, splintering bone.

Spun around by the impact, he clung to the side of the truck. Out the corner of his eye, he saw the other combat droids moving to form a semicircle in front of him.

He fought the rising tide of pain and dragged the autopistol up, finger gripping the trigger.

The droids opened fire as one, the power of their combined weaponry literally tearing George Takagi's body to bloody shreds.

As the shooting ceased, one droid crouched beside the sodden body and checked the pulse. Satisfied, the droid stood up, gesturing sharply. Its head tilted, the droid listened intently.

"They're coming," it snapped. The voice was flat, lacking inflection, and had a metallic edge to it.

The strike team fell back into the shadows, where they reloaded their weapons and waited.

For their second kill of the evening....

1

"You know what I hate about this damn city," Cade said irritably, wheeling the battered cruiser along Eleventh Avenue. It wasn't a question, really. Just a statement. "It can't make up its mind. One minute its rain, rain, rain. Next a godawful heat wave."

He glanced across at Janek. The cybo sat cool and calm in his seat, swaying to the roll of the speeding car. His white-blond head moved in time to the jazz playing inside his skull.

"Why couldn't I get a partner who likes guns? Or women? What do I get? The only cybo jazz freak on the damn force."

Cade reached across and tapped his partner on the shoulder. Janek glanced across at him, smiling indulgently.

"You're getting cranky again, T.J.," he said in his most soothing tone. "Is it the job getting to you?"

"The job's fine," Cade snapped. "It isn't the job. It's my partner."

"Who, me?" Janek looked innocent. "Paranoia also. You should talk to Abby."

Dr. Abigail Landers was the head of the Cybo Tech facility in New York, the same facility that had created and built Janek. Since a session in the facility some months back, due to superficial damage sustained during an investigation, Janek had paid a number of visits to the facility, where Dr. Landers had been conducting interface sessions with the cybo. She was interested in his developing personality traits and was conducting an in-depth study.

Janek's visits were giving him big ideas, Cade regularly told him. That was not the kind of thing that was about to help his career in the Justice Department.

"Worst thing that ever happened," Cade said. "Meeting that woman."

"Your trouble, Thomas, is jealousy. I'm becoming smarter all the time, and you just can't stand that."

Cade didn't even answer.

Staring through the windshield, Janek said, "What's so important that Takagi needs us out tonight?"

"Search me," Cade replied. "All I can tell you is he sounded scared. And that's not George."

"Maybe he owes somebody money."

"No. George doesn't gamble. It's something stronger than that."

The more he thought about it, the more intense his worrying became. It nagged at him as he pushed the cruiser downtown, silently cursing the thronged traffic.

He was still worrying when he wheeled the cruiser along the fringes of Battery Park, looking out for Takagi's 4x4. He spotted it parked exactly where George had said it would be.

Cade jammed on the brakes and brought the cruiser to a noisy halt.

"Hey!" Janek said. "Easy on the pedal, partner. I nearly totaled the windshield."

Cade reached for the SPAS shotgun clamped between the seats. He checked it for a full tube, slipping a handful of spare cartridges into his pocket, then repeated the move with his Magnum autopistol.

"I don't see any Indians," Janek murmured, staring into the gloom. "Why the panic?"

"Because of them," Cade said, indicating the dark shapes of the combat droids fanning out from the cover of Takagi's truck.

His words were punctuated by the crackle of autofire as the droids opened up. The cruiser began to shudder under the impact. The windshield blew in, filling the compartment with fragments.

"Here we go again," Janek said, kicking open his door and rolling out of the car.

Cade did likewise, diving clear as the cruiser was stitched along its length. He tucked the SPAS under his body as he cleared the side of the vehicle. He got to his knees, brought the shotgun to his shoulder and triggered a couple of shots at the closest droid. The combat shotgun's powerful charge blasted the droid's head, enough of the shot getting through the eye sockets to enter the electronic brain. The droid reacted drastically. It ran full tilt into the side of the cruiser, skidding across the hood to crash to the ground on the far side.

Even while Cade was handling the first droid, Janek picked out his own target. His heavy autopistol, free of its holster, tracked in on the advancing combat droid. Janek loosed two shots, each finding its mark. The droid's eyes exploded as the bullets penetrated, coring through to the brain and dumping it on the ground like so much scrap metal.

"Behind you!" Cade yelled, straightening up and tracking the SPAS on the figure of the surviving droid that was angling toward Janek.

The instant Cade triggered the SPAS, the combat droid opened up with its submachine gun. A hail of slugs caught Janek in the back, knocking him off balance.

Cade's blast whacked the droid in the side of the head. The toughened casing resisted the impact, and the droid swiveled around to lock its autoweapon in on the Justice cop.

Cade took a long dive to the ground, then rolled as he landed, hearing the rattle of slugs from the SMG pounding the earth around him. He paused long enough to spot the droid reloading the SMG, and lunged upright. Lifting the shotgun, Cade began triggering as fast as he was able, pumping shot after shot at the droid's expressionless face. The droid let out an odd screech of sound, throwing its arms skyward. Arching back, it fell to the ground, performing a series of ugly, spasmodic movements before its damaged brain shut down.

Janek joined Cade. "I owe you one, T.J.," he said.

"I'll remember," Cade promised, not looking up from his task. He was thumbing fresh loads into the SPAS.

Janek glanced toward the sky. "I think we have something else to worry about, T.J."

Moments later the Skorpion helicopter came burning down out of the night sky, and shells from a 50 mm belly gun chopped the earth around the Justice cops. They made a break in different directions, then turned to return fire as the chopper hissed by them. It began taking a hard turn, angling around in a tight circle.

Cade thumbed in the final cartridge and worked the shotgun's slide, cocking the weapon. He snapped the butt to his shoulder as the Skorpion wheeled about. The pilot brought it in low, seeking his targets as he powered the sleek chopper forward.

Cade stood his ground, arcing the SPAS in a line that followed the chopper's course, and waited his chance.

A few yards away, sideways to the helicopter, Janek brought his autopistol up in a two-handed grip. His keen eyes fixed on the blurred shape of the pilot behind the Plexiglas canopy, and he quickly calculated speed and trajectory before he aimed and triggered, emptying his magazine into the pilot's cabin.

The Plexiglas blew apart and the Skorpion veered off course as the pilot's head abruptly disintegrated.

Cade let go with the SPAS then, hitting the canopy from the front. The secondary blast from the shotgun, unhampered by the Plexiglas, took the pilot's already shattered head nearly off his shoulders.

Already lifeless, the pilot's hands slipped from the controls, while his feet became deadweight on the foot pedals. The Skorpion went into a steep climb, starting to turn in a complete circle.

That was when Cade hit it again, this time driving his four shots into the chopper's underbelly. He hit the fuel tank, and the combat machine erupted in a screeching ball of fire. The air filled with flying debris and burning fuel. Covered in flame, the bulk of the chopper sank to earth with a loud crash. Flames and sparks boiled skyward.

Janek ejected the empty clip from his autopistol, pulled a fresh one from his coat and snapped it into place. He worked the slide, cocking the weapon as he crossed to where Cade stood watching the burning wreck.

"Remind me not to take late-night strolls in the park with you again," Janek said dryly. He gestured in the direction of the downed droids. "You know what they are, don't you? Combat droids."

"Yeah, I know. Military use only," Cade said. "So what the hell did they and George Takagi have in common?"

"Something to do with what he needed to talk about?"

"Yeah, it seems the only answer. Too much of a co-incidence to be otherwise."

"I'll call this in," Janek said. "You going to look for George?"

Cade nodded. He wasn't too hopeful that he would find anything pleasant. The odds on Takagi's being alive were slim, taking into account the reception committee that had been waiting for Cade and Janek.

He found the NYPD tech on the far side of the 4x4. Takagi had been chopped to ribbons by heavy autofire.

For a minute Cade just stood looking down at him, feeling anger swell inside while some other emotion made his eyes sting and his throat feel tight. He swore softly, then crouched beside the body to check Takagi's pockets. There was nothing out of the ordinary. Whatever the tech had wanted to talk about had been inside his head, and that knowledge had died with him. Unless Cade could backtrack and pick up a lead.

Besides, Cade had a personal stake in this. Takagi had been a friend asking for help, and Cade didn't like letting friends down. He was puzzled, too, by the involvement of military combat droids and a military helicopter.

Just what the hell had George Takagi unearthed?

It had been enough to get him killed, and it had almost had the same effect on Cade and Janek.

Janek came up behind him, casting a quick glance at Takagi's remains.

"The cleanup crews are on their way," he reported. "George must have learned something pretty heavy to bring all this down on him."

"That's the way I see it," Cade said, straightening up. "You probably want to take a look at those droids, see if they have any kind of ID on them. Might give us a lead to where they came from."

"What are you going to do?"

Cade pulled a cigar from his pocket and proceeded to light it. "I'm going to have a goddamn smoke," he said. "And the hell with you and your fussing."

Janek crouched beside one of the droids. He checked it for signs of functioning but found nothing. The destruction of the intricate electronic brain had terminated the droid. A faint ripple of unease ran through Janek. He was aware of his own vulnerability and realized *he* could be lying where the droid was.

Pushing aside the negative thoughts, Janek examined the droid. His sensitive fingertips located the access panel in the armored torso, just under the left arm. It was a touch panel, operated by a simple pressure code. Janek's fingers found the pressure spots, and the panel slid open. Inside was a control unit that allowed technicians to expose the droid's inner functions. Janek focused on the row of tiny figures stamped on the plate and memorized them.

He repeated the check on the other droids. By this time he could hear the distant wail of sirens. Returning to where Cade stood beside George Takagi's body, he glanced up in time to see the first of the local patrol vehicles arriving.

A pair of uniformed police officers climbed out of their cruiser, and made their way across to Cade.

"T.J., that you?" one of the patrolmen asked.

"Hello, Mac."

"What the hell went down here?"

"We've got a dead cop here," Cade replied. "And the perps spread around the area."

"Hey, these are combat droids," Mac's partner said. "On the fuckin' streets? What gives?"

"Right now we don't know," Janek said. "But we're going to find out."

More vehicles began to roll in. The darkness became crisscrossed with flashing blue-and-red lights. Overhead an NYPD air cruiser slid out of the night sky.

"Jesus," Mac said. "This is George Takagi. What did those mothers do to him?"

"What I want to know is *why*," Cade said. "Mac, you make sure they treat George right."

He crossed to the bullet-riddled cruiser and climbed in. Janek followed. Glass rattled from the door frame as he slammed it shut, then Cade fired up the engine and rolled the cruiser away from the scene of the crime.

"Where?" Janek asked. "No, let me guess. NYPD headquarters? George's office?"

Cade hit the street, shoving his foot hard down on the gas pedal. The abused cruiser groaned in protest, and wind howled in through the glassless windshield.

"Every machine I ever deal with does nothing but moan."

Janek looked hurt, deciding that Cade was including him in that remark. He settled back in his seat, tuning in to one of New York's all-night jazz stations. The music filled his head, washing away the troubled world, and he felt a measure of contentment taking over after his earlier uneasy mood.

The NYPD headquarters building, a massive steel-and-glass block on the Civic Center site, even boasted a helipad on its roof. It had been rebuilt twice since the turn of the century. This time, the designers claimed, they had it right.

Cade rolled the creaking cruiser to a stop outside the main entrance. Before he could climb out, a KC-200 patrol droid appeared at his door.

"I'm sorry, sir, but I'll have to ask you to move your vehicle. No unauthorized parking within the yellow zone."

Cade flashed his badge. "Want to think again?"

The KC straightened up. "Of course, Marshal Cade."

The main lobby was crowded. Uniformed cops, human and droid, came and went in a constant stream. Behind the long booking area, banks of TV screens relayed information and showed news updates of the night's criminal activity.

Cade knew where Takagi's office was situated. It was on the twelfth floor. The express elevator rose as if it was preparing for lift-off. It deposited them on the twelfth floor.

Most of the offices were deserted, and they walked along dim, near-silent corridors. Takagi's office was in darkness except for the glow coming from the monitor on his computer desk. The office itself was neat, tidy almost to the extreme. Takagi, brilliant as he was with his computer, had also retained the Japanese obsession for order. Even the pens on the desk lay in line.

Cade stepped into the office, glancing at the blank monitor as he bent over to switch on the desk lamp.

"Can we get a printout of what's been going through the system today?" he asked.

Immediately Janek reached for the keyboard and tapped in a few commands. Moments later the laser

printer clicked on. Paper began to slide from the slot.
Janek gathered the sheet and passed it to Cade.

The printout listed all the operations since the computer had been switched on that morning. It gave times
for each separate operation. The day's listing was all
fairly straightforward, indicating that Takagi had been
busy with an analysis program, gathering information
for a statistical report. There was nothing out of the
ordinary until late evening. Then there had been a flurry
of activity, including data sent out via a phone modem, a block of information transferred to another
computer, and some time later that same information
wiped from Takagi's computer.

"The time schedule is close to when George called
you and fixed the meet," Janek observed, indicating the
figures printed over each operation.

Before they had the chance to study the sheet in detail, the door of Takagi's office swung open, showing a
figure framed in the opening.

Cade folded the printout and slipped it into his
pocket.

"Who the hell are you? And what are you doing in
this office?"

"T. J. Cade, Justice Department. This is my partner, Marshal Janek." Cade held out his badge.

The big man in the doorway took the leather badge
wallet and examined the shield carefully. He took his
time before he handed it back to Cade.

Janek, watching the man, realized that his eyes were
anywhere but on the badge. The man was stalling for
time, the cybo realized. Gathering his thoughts.

"I'm Captain Barney Culver. You want to tell me
why you're here? You understand I can't have just anyone walking around the department, Cade."

"*You* understand something, Culver. *I* don't need to justify myself to you, or anyone in this building. Right now I'm investigating a homicide. George Takagi was shot to death in Battery Park less than an hour ago."

Culver made a good stab at looking shocked. "You got to be mistaken. I was talking to George earlier. Then I sent him home. Told him to go because he'd been overworking. That was the last I saw of him. What the hell was he doing in Battery Park?"

Cade saw no point in concealing Takagi's reason for being in the park. Culver would find out once the news got around about the killing...if he didn't already know.

"He was supposed to be meeting me. He called and we arranged to meet. It sounded urgent. When we got there, George was already dead but his killers were still around."

"Did you stop them?" Culver asked.

"Permanently," Janek said. "But the odd thing was who they were."

"Someone you knew?"

"They were combat droids. Military hardware."

Culver forced a thin smile. "Combat droids in Battery Park? You sure about that?"

"Hard to make a mistake over an armored combat droid," Cade said, his voice heavy with sarcasm. "They tend to stand out in a crowd."

"Look, Cade, I find all this hard to believe. Why would combat droids be on the lookout for George Takagi? For Christ's sake, he never even did any military service. So there's no connection."

"There's a connection," Cade said. "Right now it's not very clear, but it's there."

"And we'll find it," Janek added helpfully.

"You said you spoke to George before he left," Cade went on. "What did you discuss? Anything he might have been worried about?"

Culver shook his head emphatically. "No, there was nothing specific. We just chewed the fat a little, then I suggested he take a break and go home. He worked too hard. George's problem was his lack of family. Outside the office he didn't have much to occupy him. If I'd let him, he would have bunked down next to his damn computer. Don't get me wrong. He was a good tech. We'll all miss him."

Cade turned to leave, but at the door he paused, and Janek nearly collided with him.

"I might need to talk to you again, Culver—be available."

Janek stayed silent until they were in the elevator and dropping rapidly to the ground floor. "Well?" he demanded sharply. "Okay, I'll say it. He was lying, T.J."

"Through his goddamn teeth," Cade said. "That son of a bitch knew George was dead. And I have a sneaking feeling he expected us to be, as well."

"Whatever George found, he took to Culver," Janek suggested. "Culver told him to forget it and go home, but George called you and arranged to meet."

"You can bet your ass Culver listened to George's call, then contacted whoever he's in with and arranged for those droids to trail George and deal with him."

"George walked right into it. He wouldn't have stood a chance," Janek said.

"We were supposed to be the supporting act," Cade said, "to make sure everyone was out of the picture."

"Why, T.J.? What was it George had to tell you?"

"I don't know, partner. Except it was strong enough to get him blown away."

2

The droid in charge of the Justice Department car pool wandered around the cruiser, shaking its head and making disapproving sounds. It carried a clipboard in one chrometal hand and kept making notes.

"You handle this," Cade said. "I have to get up to the office."

"You know how I hate dealing with this kind of thing," Janek protested. "This droid is a jerk. It makes me beg forgiveness every time I come in with a dented cruiser. I think it believes the cost comes out of his salary."

"What salary? It's a service droid, Janek. They work for nothing. Not like you."

"If it had its shirt blown off its back every time it went out, it'd need a salary," the cybo complained bitterly. "Have you seen the mess those combat droids made of my jacket?"

Cade nodded. "They ought to make you wear disposable overalls. No appreciation of decent clothes."

"I'd hardly call *you* a man of fashion," Janek said as Cade left him and headed for the elevator.

Braddock, the department commander, called Cade across as he entered the office. "Hear you had a busy evening, T.J."

Braddock was a big man with a genuinely friendly face and a manner to match. He was an ex-Chicago cop, and he'd been with the department for close to ten years.

"It got that way," Cade said. He helped himself to a mug of coffee from the department pot. He was aware of Braddock watching him closely.

"And—?"

Braddock grinned. "Can't keep anything from you, can I, hotshot?"

"Somebody been making waves?"

"Yes. Local cop named Culver. He claims you've been into his department without authorization. Poking around. And you gave him a hard time."

Cade drank some more coffee as he digested the information. He liked what he was hearing. It meant Culver was agitated enough to try to cover himself by making a fuss.

"He's right on all three counts," Cade said, "and I may be going back to give him a harder time if I get the right answers to some questions."

"Is he bent?" Braddock asked.

"Let's say that at the moment he has a slight list to starboard."

Braddock chuckled. The sound was deep, coming from way down in his chest. "Good enough, T.J. Just watch your back."

"Tell *him* that," Cade said as Janek appeared.

Janek ignored the remark and went past the two men. Braddock spotted the shredded jacket and shirt.

"Hey, Janek, didn't they teach you how to duck at Cybo Tech?"

The cybo paused at the door to the office. He glanced at Braddock, then slowly raised his right hand, the second finger stiffly erect in a gesture of defiance.

"Sit on this, Braddock," he said tautly.

Grinning, Braddock turned to Cade. "You teach him that?"

Cade shook his head. "I think he picked it up from watching you."

"Yeah? You know, that boy's got good taste, after all."

Cade closed the office door and sat down at his desk. He checked the vid-phone recorder for messages. It was blank.

"I'll run some background checks on Culver," Janek said. He had discarded his ripped jacket and shirt, pulling on a roll-neck sweater from the locker in the corner of the room. "See if I can come up with anything. And I'll throw in the ID numbers from the combat droids."

The vid-phone rang, and Cade picked up the receiver. He watched the blank screen light up, and Kate Bannion's face appeared.

"Hi," she said. "I'm looking for a smart cop."

"Sorry, miss, I'm all that's available."

"You'll have to do."

"Is this purely a social call? Or are you on official business?"

"Both," Kate replied, giving him one of her smiles. "I just got back from an assignment and I wanted to see you. But I also found a message on my recorder for you. It's from George Takagi, T.J., and it sounds important."

"Damn!" Cade resisted saying anything else. He stared at Kate's image on the screen. "Stay put. I'm on my way over. Don't answer the door to anyone but me. Understand?"

Kate nodded, astute enough to realize something had to be wrong if Cade was acting in such a manner.

He broke the connection, dropping the receiver. He pulled the computer readout from George Takagi's office and searched for something. Kate's phone number was there. He'd missed it when Barney Culver had come into the office. Reaching in the drawer of his desk, he picked up a number of fresh clips for his .357 Magnum autopistol. Dropping them in his pocket, he called to Janek. "Grab your hat, partner, we're on our way out. I have a feeling we just got our break."

"Break? What break?" Janek questioned as he followed Cade out the office and through to the elevator.

"Kate just called. While she was out, George Takagi left a recorded message on her vid-phone. It was on that damn readout we took from George's computer."

They reached the basement. Janek retrieved the SPAS and spare shells from the wrecked cruiser. He indicated a sleek, six-month-old Ford.

"You got that out of old tight-ass?" Cade asked as he slid into the passenger seat.

Janek fired up the supercharged vehicle, giving his partner a sly grin. "Hell, no, but who gives a damn?"

He freed the brake and dropped the car into gear. It shot forward, burning rubber as the cybo floored the pedal. The droid came out of its cubicle, waving its skinny chrometal arms as the car roared by him. It hit the exit ramp, leaving a trail of bright sparks in its wake. At the head of the ramp Janek executed a sharp left turn, gunning the engine as he forced his way into the traffic. Horns blared and tires screeched in protest as drivers stood on their brakes, but Janek ignored them. He pushed the Ford to the limit, with the siren howling and red light flashing.

"Have you been sniffing brake fluid or something?" Cade asked incredulously.

"You do want to get to Kate's in a hurry, don't you?"

"Hell, yes, but I want to be alive when I get there. Preferably with dry pants."

"Trust me, T.J., I can handle it."

"Remind me to have a word with Abby Landers," Cade said. "Time she started cooling you down."

"Abby told me I have to be natural. Act on the spur of the moment."

"Yeah? You remind her I'm the sucker who has to sit next to you when one of these moments takes hold."

Cade resigned himself to their erratic drive, and they reached Kate's apartment block in record time. Janek swung into the basement parking area, and they took the elevator up.

"Kate, it's me," Cade said, activating the door-vid.

Kate unlocked the door and let them in.

"What's all this about, T.J.?" she asked.

"George is dead," Cade said. "He called saying he wanted to meet me. Said he had something to tell me. We got there too late."

"Soon enough to almost get our asses shot off," Janek grumbled as he locked the door.

"T.J., I'm sorry about George. He was a nice guy."

"Where's the message?"

Kate slid the tape into her VCR, and moments later George Takagi's face appeared on the TV screen.

"That's his office he's calling from," Janek observed, then they all listened silently to a man who was no longer alive.

"Hi, Kate. I want you to get this to T.J. as soon as you can. I'm going to call him for a meeting, so if everything goes as planned we won't need this. If things go wrong, at least he'll have this to use.

"I pulled some info from the computer tonight, and I have a feeling there's something odd going on. Can't explain why. Maybe it's just my mystical Japanese ancestry coming through—ho, ho.

"I have three dead people, all killed in exactly the same way and within days of each other. Now the odd part. They all worked for the same company. The Amosin Corporation. And somebody tried to lose their death reports in the computer system. Thing is, you can't erase death reports. They are automatically filed. So they were pushed into an obscure corner until my retrieval system accidently pulled them back out.

"Maybe I'm chasing shadows, but I have a feeling something stinks. I see a cover-up. Right now I don't have anything else to go on except good old gut feeling.

"T.J., I know you won't let this go. I'm going to bring my boss, Barney Culver, into the picture. I can't handle this by myself.

"I'm keying in the modem now, and it will send you a copy of the files I picked up. See you soon, guys."

Takagi's image was erased by static, then the computer clicked in and relayed the files Takagi had mentioned. They showed the three death reports, followed by computer files on the three dead people.

"He must have called me shortly after," Cade said. "Couldn't mention what it was about over the phone."

"You say he was dead when you arrived?" Kate asked. "Then someone must have overheard his conversation with you and arranged for his killers to be at the location. That's fast work, T.J."

"Has to be someone in the department," Janek said. "And I put my money on Culver."

"From what George said, Culver was the guy he was going to contact. If Culver is involved, he'd have been in a good position to tap in on George's calls. George calls me, Culver calls his hit squad and they trail George to the meeting place. Take him out and wait for us."

"But why?" Kate asked. "What's so important about the deaths of three people from Amosin? Why kill George and try to kill you?"

"If I had the answer that fast, I'd be chief of police," Cade said.

Janek shook his head. "You'd look terrible in the uniform."

"Cut the comedy and get that expensive brain of yours cranked up to figure this deal out."

"See what I have to put up with, Kate?" Janek said, looking for sympathy. "There are times when he treats me like a machine."

"I'm finding you more and more—how shall I put this?—all too human. Quit being a nuisance, or I'll trade you in for a new model. One without an attitude."

"What damn attitude? I don't have an attitude, Thomas."

"Let's get the show on the road, Janek."

The cybo sat down, his gaze fixed on the TV screen where Takagi's computer readout was still displayed.

"The three Amosin employees worked in the same division of the company," he said. "They were in the robotics division. Military contracts department. That would mean work for the Department of Defense. The droids who killed George were combat machines built and supplied for the military. Give you odds those droids turn out to be Amosin models."

"That chopper we took out was a Skorpion," Cade added, peering at the screen. "Military use only."

Janek gave a pleased smile. "It is amazing what even you can come up with when you try, T.J."

"Hey, quit arguing, you guys," Kate protested.

Cade straightened up. "Who's arguing?"

"Just a lively debate," Janek agreed.

Kate shook her head, smiling at them. "You two are a pair. You squabble just like siblings—adolescent siblings, at that."

"Adolescent?" Janek repeated huffily.

"Yeah, Janek, just don't forget that women love to feel superior to men." Cade paused to grin at Kate, then went on. "So how do you read this stuff?"

"If Culver is involved, he must have acted fast to get those droids out after George. Okay, he panicked and went for overkill, but he was still able to round up help in a short time."

"He's got local help, in other words," Cade said. "Military hardware."

"Narrows the field down," Kate said. "Should be easy enough to get the military to make a check on any missing hardware. Shouldn't it?"

Cade frowned and ran his hand through his hair. "Trouble is, we don't know who we're dealing with. If we're bucking some high-ranking guy, we could just hit a blank wall. The military has an old habit of closing ranks when civilians start asking questions. We're going to have to do this the sneaky way."

"Why are you looking at me?" Janek asked.

"Run your checks on those droids. If you come up with any military tag numbers, see if you can pin them down with ComNet."

"Hah!" Janek said. He twisted around, fixing his gaze on Cade. "Now you want me to break into the military computer network. What next, T.J.? Fraud? Extortion? No please or thank you. Just break the law, Janek, it's all in the name of justice."

"You finished already? Good. Now, do you think you can do it?"

Janek looked hurt. "Can I do it? Can a cat lick it's own—"

"I get the picture. So let's get back to the office."

Cade took the video from Kate's VCR.

"You don't know a damn thing about this, Kate. Forget the tape. We were never here tonight. When you hear about George's death, you'll be surprised and upset. And if anyone starts asking questions, you play dumb. It might even be a good idea if you skipped town for a few days."

"No way, T.J. I'm not running away."

"Listen. Your number was on a readout we took from George's computer. If we could find it, so could somebody else. I don't want you in the line of fire, Kate."

"I'll be careful. If I get worried, I'll call you."

Cade knew better than to argue. Kate Bannion was as stubborn as she was beautiful.

"Make sure you do."

She nodded, then said, "Hey, *you* be careful, T.J. Don't get yourself in too deep."

He kissed her, holding onto her for a moment.

"I'll be careful, too," Janek muttered as he followed Cade to the door.

Kate grinned. "Watch out for those cute little microchips, Janek."

"Come on, partner," Cade said. "Quit mooning and let's get back to the office...."

As soon as Janek was settled before his computer bank, Cade headed for the door.

"Where will you be if I need you?" Janek asked.

"I'm going to keep a watch on Culver. Sooner or later he's going to contact somebody, and I'd like to be around when he does."

"We're going to look like a couple of idiots if we're wrong about him."

"He's our man," Cade said. "I feel it in my bones."

3

Cade leaned forward, easing the ache in his back. He glanced at his watch. It was almost 8:00 a.m., but the heat was already building up. Above the roofs of the buildings, he caught a glimpse of the hard blue sky.

He glanced at Culver's apartment building. The cop's car was still in its parking slot where Culver had left it when he'd arrived home just after midnight. Cade had been in his car, across the street, watching ever since.

Now he saw a long black limousine slide silently up behind Culver's vehicle. The limo looked out of place on the street. Cade made a note of its registration plates, then picked up the handset and punched in the office number.

"T.J.?"

"Run a make on this registration number," Cade said.

"Give me a couple of minutes," Janek replied. "Is something happening?"

"No. I've just decided to start collecting registration numbers. Everyone should have a hobby."

"Yeah? I've got a human for mine," the cybo said dryly.

Barney Culver stepped out of his building. He was in a hurry. Without pause he went straight to the waiting limo and climbed in the back. The moment he'd closed the door, the limo pulled away from the curb and accelerated down the street. Cade fired up the Ford and moved ahead, careful to keep a good four car-lengths' distance.

He followed the limo through the rush-hour traffic. It was easy to keep the vehicle in sight. Traffic, as ever, was slow. New York's overcrowded streets were at saturation point. Nothing changed where traffic was concerned. The American love affair with the motor vehicle was as strong as ever. Despite the cost, the appalling driving conditions and the rapid development of aircars, people still wanted their gas-guzzling motors. There was a surfeit of oil, with the massive finds in the Arctic and the redevelopment of the Alaskan fields. There wasn't a politician in the country who would have dared suggest a cutback in car production.

Cade picked up the phone when it buzzed.

"The vehicle is registered to the Amosin Corporation," Janek said. "Now do you want to tell me what's going on?"

"Barney Culver just got picked up by this car. It called at his apartment building."

"Where's it heading?"

"Right now along Lexington Avenue. I'll let you know where we end up. Any luck with your computer search?"

"This is a tough one, T.J. I managed to pin down the numbers I took from the combat droids. They're U.S. Army code numbers. That was the easy part. The difficulty is breaking into ComNet. I'm having to take things steady in case they have some kind of alert code built in to warn if there's an unauthorized command."

"Stay with it, buddy," Cade said. "I'll get back to you."

A few minutes later the limo cut off across town, heading down toward the docks on the East River. Cade was forced to drop back even farther as the traffic thinned out. He lost sight of his target a couple of times when lumbering diesel rigs and trailers pushed their way past him. Finally tiring of playing games with one of the rigs, Cade accelerated and passed the rig just in time to catch a glimpse of the limo's taillights as it shot down a side street. Cade swore forcibly, standing on the brakes and spinning the wheel. As the car slid around, the approaching semi was forced to make a hard stop. The driver, a massive six footer, jumped from the cab and stormed up to Cade's car. He thumped a hamlike fist on the driver's window.

Cade thumbed the button, dropping the window.

"You got a problem?" Cade asked.

"No," the trucker yelled, "you got the fuckin' problem, jerk!"

Cade slipped the door catch and booted it open. The door whacked the trucker in the gut. He backpedaled, his beefy face darkening with anger. "Tough guy, huh?"

Cade held up his badge with one hand and the .357 with the other.

"You want to find out?"

The trucker read the badge and the gun, the anger still boiling in his eyes.

"Maybe I should call in the local cruiser. Get them to run a check on your rig. See how many violations we can spot."

The trucker backed off, muttering darkly. He climbed back in his cab and roared off, leaving a trail of diesel fumes behind.

Cade got back behind the wheel and swung it along the side street. There were no hidden entrances for the limo to have taken, so he assumed it had traveled the

length of the street. When he got to the far end, he saw
that the left turn reached a dead end after twenty yards,
while the right led to a dock area where a sprawling
warehouse complex stood.

The black limo was already inside the complex, rolling slowly along the dock. Cade watched it turn in at the
entrance to the last warehouse in the line. He eased the
Ford to the dock entrance. The security droid on the
gate stepped out of its hut.

"Can I help you, sir?"

Cade showed his badge. The droid's eyes scanned the
badge, picking up the bar code. The code activated a
memory chip that instructed the droid to defer to the
Justice marshal.

"Anything I can do to help, Marshal Cade?"

"No. I just need to look around. No sweat."

The droid opened the barrier and Cade drove in. He
kept his eyes open as he eased the car into a parking slot
just inside the entrance. He covered the length of the
dock on foot. There wasn't much activity. Only one
travel-stained freighter was moored against the quayside, and the robot dockworkers who were loading the
vessel ignored Cade as he passed by. He reached the far
end of the line of warehouses and saw that the huge
doors had been closed. He moved around the end wall,
checking the length of the massive building. There was
a small access door set in the wall. Cade tried the handle and found it was unlocked. He eased the door open
enough to allow him to slip through.

Once he was inside, he pressed himself against the
wall, keeping to the deep shadows thrown by the stacked
goods filling the interior. He cautiously threaded his
way across the floor area, toward the source of the

voices he could hear. It took him a couple of minutes to pin the sound down.

Peering around the edge of stacked crates, Cade spotted the black limo. It was parked in a cleared area of the floor, and a number of figures were gathered around it.

Cade recognized Barney Culver first. The cop was having an animated conversation with a tall, sandy-haired man in his early forties. The others surrounding them were all armed. The conversation between Culver and the sandy-haired man became louder. Culver looked to be getting angry.

"...give me a hard time, Tane," the cop said forcibly. "I had to do something fast. Takagi had gotten lucky picking those names out of the computer banks. If he hadn't come to me, this whole deal might be slipping down the tubes right now. We're too short on time to let complications get in the way."

"You didn't have to start a war right in the middle of Battery Park," Tane replied. "Jesus, Culver."

"Look, I figured I had to take the chance to get rid of him before he could talk to Cade. The man is a Justice marshal. Like 'em or not, they're tough bastards. Admit it, Tane, the combat droids messed up. All they had to do was ice Takagi, then wait until Cade and his partner showed and do the same for them. Instead, we ended up with a goddamn massacre...those droids totaled and that chopper of yours shot out of the sky. So don't blow your stack at me. You and your mercs were hired to handle this sort of thing. You gave me the contact for those droids in case of an emergency, and I used them."

"The colonels aren't going to be too happy about this," Tane said tightly. "They wanted us to keep a low profile until the day. Now look. *Low fuckin' profile!*"

"Don't forget it was your damn droids who terminated the three Amosin workers when they decided they wanted out of the deal," Culver said angrily. "Those shit-for-brains droids had to do each one exactly the same. No wonder Takagi got suspicious."

Culver took a deep breath.

"Okay. Okay, Tane. Let's calm down. Takagi's dead. I've done what I can to lose the data in the computer banks. The main worry now is Cade. I don't think he believed everything I told him last night. Could be he's doing some digging right now. He has a reputation for staying with something until it breaks one way or the other."

"Meaning he'll be coming back to talk to you?"

"Possibly," Culver said.

"Then we've got to take him out," Tane insisted. "But this time I'll handle it."

"What do I do? Sit around and wait for him to come looking for me? Right now I'm the only link he has to George Takagi."

"Get out of town for a few days. Use your rank to swing it. Hell, I don't know. Just vanish."

"I guess I could take the boat out for a run," Culver said. "I'm due some time."

Tane nodded. "Then do it. Give me some room to work, and I'll have this supercop, Cade, boxed and wrapped by the time you get back."

Culver nodded. He climbed back in the limo, and two of the gunmen joined him, one getting behind the wheel. Someone raised the warehouse door, and the limo backed out. The door slid shut again with an oiled rattle.

The man named Tane took a portable telephone from one of his gunmen. He tapped in a number, waiting for it to connect.

"Colonel, it's me, Tane. Yeah. We just finished speaking. What do I think? I don't trust him, sir. I didn't like the way he handled the Takagi affair. It could have been done a lot quieter. That's the trouble when you deal with the civilians, sir. They don't have the military mind to back them up. I'm going to handle things myself from now on.... Culver? You could be right, sir. We can survive without him. We have other solid connections within the police department.... Whatever you say, sir. Consider it done. And the other matter is being organized right now. We'll have everything in place in time. Right, sir. I'll be in touch."

Tane cut the connection and handed the phone back to his man. "Okay, let's get things rolling. Someone's going into early retirement, and we're going to help him along the way."

"So long, Culver!" someone said, raising a grim chuckle from the assembled gunmen.

The automatic door opened. A sleek Chrysler Centaur MK 4 with a turbo-boosted engine rolled out of the warehouse shadows. Tane and two of his men climbed in. The gleaming car nosed its silent way out of the warehouse, and the door dropped behind it.

Cade watched the remaining two mercs. They stood talking for a moment, then made their way to an office where they sat down and opened cans of beer.

Business was heating up. Cade decided it was time to do some pushing of his own. He worked his way to the rear of the office. The main wall and one side had glass panels, allowing supervision over the main warehouse area. The door was in the end wall, which had solid construction. Cade was covered right up to the moment he opened the door and entered the structure. Pressed up against the door, he could hear the muted tones of the pair inside. He pulled the .357 autopistol, easing off the safety. Reaching for the handle of the door, Cade gripped his weapon, mentally picturing the position of the two gunmen at the table.

Then he pressed the handle, shoved open the door and went in fast.

They were both still at the table. The one facing Cade had a beer can raised to his lips. The other was halfway out of his seat, already turning as he moved to carry out some errand.

He saw Cade before his partner and reacted the moment he spotted the Magnum.

Cade recognized the look in the man's eyes and knew damn well that the idiot was going to go for his gun.

He threw up his left hand in warning. "Don't try..." he yelled, knowing the guy wasn't going to pay any attention. He saw the man's fingers curl around the butt of the gun holstered under his left arm, and tracked the .357 around, pulling the trigger....

The powerful slug hit the target high in the chest on the left side. It shredded flesh and muscle as it tunneled through and blew a spongy hole as it exited. The shot man fell back across the table, scattering everything in sight, then rolled off the edge and crashed to the floor in a heap. Blood spattered the face of his partner as he scrambled back from the table in panic. His beer can flew from nerveless fingers, and his legs got tangled up in his seat. He stumbled back, yelling in surprise, balance all gone to hell, and fell against the glass panel behind him. It shattered and he was suddenly engulfed in a shower of broken glass.

Cade reached the table, shoving it aside. He reached down and scooped the shot man's gun from its holster, then turned to jam the muzzle of the Magnum into the face of the other man as he raised his head.

"Take the gun out," Cade snapped. "Do it slowly, because I've already got the feeling I want to shoot someone else today and you're at the top of my list."

The man did as he was told. He was shaken by what had happened. His face smarted badly from numerous glass cuts, and he didn't like the hard gleam in Cade's eyes.

Cade took the proffered gun. "On your feet," he said, backing away from the man. "Get your buddy into a chair."

"Jesus," the man moaned. "He's bleeding all over the place."

"What do you expect when he got shot? You always partner idiots, or are you naturally unlucky?"

Cade checked the office for a phone and spotted one on the wall. Keeping the pair under his gun, he picked up the receiver. He punched in the office number and waited until Janek's face appeared on the vid-screen.

"Do me a favor," Cade said. "Get a cleanup team down to me right away. Got a couple of perps here for the lockup. One needs a med-droid. Gunshot wound."

"Wouldn't be from a .357 Magnum, would it?" the cybo asked. "T.J., I wish you'd curb your violent tendencies."

"Just start the ball rolling, Janek, and get down here with them." Cade gave the warehouse's telephone number, knowing that Janek would have the location within a couple of minutes.

"Don't go away, T.J.," Janek said dryly.

Cade finished the call and turned his full attention back to his prisoners.

"Be a while before the cavalry arrives, boys. So we've got time to have a nice get-acquainted chat."

4

Janek had filed away all the information Cade had passed along. The cybo's electronic brain was capable of amassing endless details, all of which he could recall at a moment's notice. Even as he absorbed the information, his data store was checking to see if he already had details on any of the names and locations.

"Sorry, T.J., I don't seem to have anything on the names you gave me."

"You can check them with Washington Central when we get back."

"What did you learn from those two?" Janek asked, referring to the prisoners.

"Nothing," Cade said. "One thing I figured out for myself. They're not the local hired guns I thought they were. Those are different. These are hard-nosed types. I'd say mercs. Didn't blink an eye when I questioned them. Knew exactly how to behave."

"Keeps coming back at us," Janek said. "Combat droids. Military helicopter. Now mercs."

"And this guy Tane. He had a telephone conversation with someone he kept calling 'Colonel.'"

"So where to now?" Janek asked.

"Barney Culver," Cade said. "Before his ex-buddies dump him."

They walked out of the warehouse. A cleanup team from the department had the area cordoned off. On Cade's instruction the two prisoners were being moved to a Justice Department secure facility. Once there, they would be totally isolated. A stakeout team would stay behind, out of sight, and monitor any visitors to the warehouse. A preliminary check of the warehouse contents had uncovered a cache of military autorifles and handguns. Janek had memorized code numbers for future checking.

"Let's find the car and get out of here," Cade said. "I want you to plug yourself into the office computer. Try and get a location for this boat Culver owns."

Minutes later, as Cade pushed his way through the traffic, Janek connected himself by means of the carphone modem to the terminal back at their office. Through the sensitive fingertips of his hand, the cybo was able to communicate directly with the data banks. It was a useful facility, saving time and effort, and was only one of his inbuilt functions.

"Culver owns a forty-foot power cruiser called *The Good Life*. Moors it at the Sag Harbor Marina on Long Island."

Cade made a mental route change. He stepped on the gas pedal and sent the vehicle surging forward, hitting the button that activated the built-in siren and set the lights flashing. Drivers began to grudgingly give way under Cade's relentless onslaught. He fought his way through until he was able to pick up East Thirty-fourth Street, then hammered the Ford up to its maximum speed, weaving in and out of the traffic.

Janek took one look at the rising speedometer needle and tightened his seatbelt. He leaned back in the padded seat and tuned in to the twenty-four-hour jazz station, trying to ignore the blur of vehicles Cade was passing.

As his awareness of human sensation and emotional response developed, the cybo often saw the sense in re-

taining his robotic indifference to such things as understanding danger or risk, or placing himself in the hands
of a reckless human. A pure robot would sit and accept
without question that his human partner was driving
like a suicide pilot. Janek was unable to do that now. He
couldn't show it physically, but in all other aspects he
was *sweating*.

Cade slowed as he approached the Queens Midtown
Tunnel and hung a sharp left. He held the siren as he
pushed through the tunnel, emerging on the Long Island Expressway, which cut across Queens and Nassau
County, and then through to Long Island itself.

There was only thin traffic heading out toward the far
end of the island. The interstate highway stretched
ahead of Cade, fading in the distance. Heat waves
shimmered on the gleaming surface.

"You'd better contact the local law," Cade suggested. "Get us clearance. I don't want some eager patrolman flagging us down."

Janek picked up the phone and isolated the area fre-
quencies. He identified himself and the vehicle, then
proceded to request assistance from the zone controller.

"What's it all about, Marshal Janek?" came the
voice of the controller.

"We have reason to believe there could be a homicide attempt taking place. Until we're able to pinpoint
the target, we need a free hand."

"I want to cooperate, Marshal Janek," the controller wavered, "but . . ."

Cade reached out and took the handset.

"T. J. Cade, Justice Department. Who are you?"

"Deputy Stillman."

"Just keep your people out of the way, Stillman. I'm not asking, I'm telling. This is Justice Department business, and it takes priority over local jurisdiction. Got it? Just let your people know."

Janek took the handset back. He dropped it on its cradle.

"There was no need..." he began.

"I don't know who else is involved in this," Cade said. "What am I supposed to do? Alert every cop between here and Grand Bahama. All we need is the wrong one, and we've blown it."

"I guess you're right," Janek conceded reluctantly.

"No guesses about it."

At the intersection with County 111, Cade left the expressway, cutting through to where he could pick up State Highway 27. He was able to follow this all the way through to Bridgehampton. From there it was an easy change to the local road that took them directly to Sag Harbor. Cade kept his foot to the floor all the way, burning past every other vehicle on the highway, including the local police cruisers.

"You obviously made an impact on Stillman," Janek remarked, noting the way the cruisers ignored their passing.

"I hope that's what it means," Cade growled.

Cade slowed the cruiser as he entered Sag Harbor. The picturesque former whaling port had stayed quite true to its origins, and, beyond its concession to android labor and the electronic conveniences of the new age, stubbornly refused to be dragged any further into the twenty-first century. The old customs house, the first in New York, was still in evidence. Following the illuminated signs, Cade drove through to the harbor, then took the road along to the extended marina.

"I could spend some time here," Janek observed. He was taking in the surroundings with great interest. "The ocean has a very soothing effect, T.J."

"Maybe they knocked you together out of old submarine parts," Cade suggested.

"You're a cynical son of a bitch," the cybo replied tautly.

Cade chuckled to himself.

"Stop here," Janek said.

He climbed out of the vehicle and stood at the rail, looking out across the water.

"Culver's boat," he said, pointing across the harbor.

Cade squinted his eyes against the hard glare of the sun. The light reflecting off the water blurred his vision.

"There. Heading out toward the point," Janek said.

"Damn!" Cade said. "We missed him."

"I think someone is following him out," Janek said. "There's a powerboat in his wake."

"Bring the SPAS," Cade said.

He started down the ramp leading to the quayside. He was heading for the powerboat rentals dock. The droid in charge, clad in seaman's thick wool jersey and wearing a battered fisherman's cap, glanced up, beaming in earnest jollity.

"And what'll it be?" it asked in rolling tones.

Cade stuck his badge under the droid's nose. The android registered the bar code and responded immediately.

"Yes, Marshal?"

"Your fastest boat," Cade said.

"There," the droid said. "The *Arrow.*"

Cade and Janek scrambled aboard the craft. Passing the SPAS combat shotgun to his partner, the cybo took the controls and fired up the powerful turbo engine. He engaged the forward gear, and the long, sleek craft leaped forward, trailing a spume of white froth in its wake. Janek settled comfortably into the synthetic leather seat, snapping the safety belt around his waist as he powered the boat up to maximum speed. Next to him, Cade was checking the SPAS's loads, cocking the weapon in readiness.

The powerboat trailing Culver's craft maintained its distance. Looking beyond the pair of vessels, Cade saw the cutoff point approaching. Once beyond the natural spit of land jutting out from the coast, they would be in the open water of Gardiners Bay. The ideal place to make a hit.

"T.J., off to the north," Janek said. "There's a chopper coming in."

Cade picked it up. Still a speck, but definitely on a course that would bring it over Culver's craft.

"What do you think?" Janek asked above the howl of the engine. "They could take out Culver's boat by themselves. Why the powerboat?"

"Maybe they need to get on board first," Cade answered. "Could be Culver has something they need to take with them.... Hell, I don't know, Janek."

The pursuing powerboat began to close in on Culver's craft as it cleared the point. The New York cop, perhaps suddenly realizing he was being chased, opened his throttles and the cruiser surged ahead, but its limited speed was no match for the powerboat. The craft accelerated and came alongside, armed figures leaping for the low deck rails.

"Let's move!" Cade yelled.

Janek added the final burst of speed that took their powerboat in a direct line for the craft attacking Culver's.

A sudden deafening roar filled the air, and the dark shape of the helicopter came at them in a long, low dive. It skimmed the surface of the water, the rotor wash whipping up white froth.

There was a heavy chatter of noise, and the water around Cade and Janek erupted in spumy geysers. Something whacked against the foredeck of the powerboat, tearing a ragged hole in the fiberglass hull.

"Move it!" Cade yelled.

Janek swung the wheel, ramming the powerboat against the craft that had attached itself to the side of Culver's vessel.

Cade spotted a dark-clad figure half-risen from the pilot's seat of the other powerboat. The man was leaning over the back of his seat, hanging on to the wheel with one hand and leveling an Army-issue autorifle. Without a second's thought, Cade brought the SPAS around and touched the trigger. The heavy blast from the combat weapon at such close range made the man's head disintegrate. He sagged back across the passenger seat, spilling his blood across the expensive upholstery.

Without waiting, Cade unclipped his belt and stood up. He took a couple of long strides across the width of the opposition's powerboat and grabbed for the cruiser's rail.

He could hear someone shouting in anger, then the sound of autofire.

He cleared the rail, hitting the cruiser's deck in a crouch, the SPAS at the ready. A gun fired close by, and slugs clanged off the rail inches from his head. Cade twisted, the muzzle of the SPAS seeking its target. He spotted a lean black man leaning out from behind the deck structure, trying for a clearer shot. Cade triggered the shotgun, twice, then again. The charge ripped away the wood from the hatchway, blasting splinters into the man's face. He stumbled away from cover, clawing at his lacerated, bleeding face. Cade fired again, this time catching his adversary between the shoulders and catapulting him along the deck in a spray of red.

Janek appeared at the rail, his handgun out. He took off along the deck, in the opposite direction to Cade, and between them they closed in on the wheelhouse. They still heard the exchange of fire, and glass blew out of a window above Cade, showering him with glittering splinters.

He heard Janek's gun firing. Single, methodical shots, and he knew that each would be finding its target.

Cade went up the companionway to the wheelhouse. A bloody figure stumbled from the open door, still holding the Army autorifle. Cade hit him with a single shot from the SPAS and blew him off his feet. Then he dropped to a crouch and went in through the door.

The interior looked like a slaughterhouse.

It *was* a slaughterhouse.

Barney Culver lay in a crumpled, blood-soaked heap near the cruiser's wheel. He had been shot to ribbons. On the opposite side lay two of the boarders. Each man had been shot directly between the eyes, the powerful soft-nosed slugs from Janek's handgun blowing off the backs of their skulls during exit.

"See if you can do anything for him," Cade yelled. He was thumbing fresh loads into the SPAS, conscious of the chopper's presence.

He moved around to the front of the wheelhouse in time to see the helicopter sliding in sideways. The hatch was open, and a couple of armed men were preparing to drop to the cruiser's deck.

Cade raised the shotgun and pumped out shot after shot. First he targeted the armed men, hitting one and driving the other back into cover. Then he switched his aim, blasting at the tail rotor. His fire took effect. The chopper began to swing off course. The pilot, aware of what Cade *could* do if he got lucky, decided on caution. He swung the chopper around and began to ease it away from the cruiser. Cade dropped the empty SPAS, pulled his .357 and began to fire with that. The Magnum slugs chewed nervously at the chopper's fuselage, and a couple through the Plexiglas canopy finally convinced the pilot he was putting it all on the line. The chopper swept away, skimming the waves as it retreated.

Cade reloaded his handgun and shotgun before he went back inside the wheelhouse.

Janek looked up from where he was crouching beside Barney Culver's body. His hands and clothing were bloodstained.

"Sorry, T.J.," he apologized. "I couldn't do a thing for him. He's dead."

JANEK WATCHED the air ambulance hover over the quayside as it came about, then it slid forward over the rooftops of Sag Harbor and vanished from sight. An interested crowd of onlookers was being kept behind the police barriers by local cops. Turning away, Janek made his way back along the deck of Culver's cruiser, stepping through the hatchway and down to the main cabin.

"Anything?" he asked.

Cade shook his head without looking up from the desk he was searching.

"I don't even know *what* I'm looking for."

Janek joined his partner and together they stripped the cabin, searching every possible place. It took over half an hour. By the end Cade was getting edgy. Janek continued, doggedly going over each section. He finally sat back on one of the padded bench seats and stared around the cabin.

"I still believe you were right, T.J. If they'd just wanted Culver dead, the chopper could have blown him out of the water."

"So what did he have on board they wanted so damn bad?"

"Evidence that might link them to whatever they're planning?"

"Insurance, you mean? Culver making certain he had something to use against them if the game got tricky?"

Janek nodded. He stood up, crossed the cabin and bent over a pile of papers scattered across the top of Culver's desk.

"Something?" Cade asked, joining the cybo.

"Could be," Janek said. "I spotted it in among the other papers, but it didn't register at the time. Not until we started talking about insurance."

"This better be good," Cade said.

"Man of little faith," Janek muttered. "Get ready to acknowledge my genius."

He straightened up, clutching a slip of paper in his hand.

"So?" Cade asked.

"This is a rental slip from the Sag Harbor Bank. Rental for a safe-deposit box. Don't you think it odd that Culver has a box in a small-town bank quite a distance from where he spends his normal working days?"

"Where people are concerned, Janek, nothing is ever odd," Cade said.

"Fine. No reason why he shouldn't have a box," Janek agreed. "But what for? Unless it's something he wants away from prying eyes. Like payoff money perhaps. Or incriminating evidence he doesn't want his partners in crime to know about?"

"Okay, Sherlock," Cade said, "let's go talk to the Sag Harbor Bank."

THE DROID behind the bank counter had a comforting smile on its satin chrome face.

"May I be of assistance?" it asked, eagerness oozing from every joint.

Janek placed the rental slip on the counter and his badge next to it.

"All very interesting," the droid said. The smile remained in place. "However, it doesn't tell me what you require."

"We need to see what's in the man's deposit box," Janek explained. "The owner has been murdered, and we are conducting an official investigation."

"The regulations state . . ."

Janek shook his head. "Not what I want to hear, friend. Now let's not get into playing games." He tapped the badge left lying on the counter. "No use pretending you don't recognize that. Justice Department. Gives us priority over your rules and regulations."

"This is all highly irregular," the droid said. Now its tone was high, starting to become tight and prissy.

"He's going to blow," Cade said over Janek's shoulder.

"T.J., it'll be fine."

But Janek wasn't too convinced himself. The droid was exhibiting that look, the one that warned it was teetering on the brink. Janek hated dealing with the limited intelligence of the dedicated service droids. Once they were confronted by a situation outside their program, they were liable to react unfavorably.

"Just call your supervisor," Janek suggested. "I'll discuss this with him or her."

The droid relaxed. Janek had offered it an easy way out. Responsibility could be passed to a superior, leaving the droid to carry on with its normal functions.

The supervisor was a tall, confident blonde. She inspected the credentials Cade and Janek presented and examined the rental slip.

"You say Captain Culver is dead?"

"He was killed a short while ago out on the bay," Cade said.

"We heard shooting. Were you involved?" she asked, looking at the bloodstains on Janek's clothing.

Cade nodded. "Culver was under investigation."

The blonde digested the news. "I see. Are you saying there might be evidence in the safe-deposit box?"

"It's possible. If there is, we need to see it now."

"You have no objection to me checking the validity of your badges?"

"Go ahead."

The blonde walked off across the administration area. Cade watched her, his eyes giving away his inner thoughts.

"Strength of character flies out the window when a tight skirt comes along, Thomas," Janek observed.

Cade grinned. "I was only looking. It's just harmless fun."

Janek frowned. "I thought sex was a serious business?"

"What the hell are you talking about?"

Janek started to say "I was..." but just then the blonde returned to hand back their badges.

"They check out. It appears you are genuine. Under the circumstances, I believe we can waive the regulations. If you would follow me..."

She led the way to the elevator, which shot them down to the basement where the vaults were located. Security droids manned all the entrances and exits. The vault area was decorated in soothing whites and pastel shades, with concealed, soft lighting.

"I thought this was for people to look at their money," Janek said. "This is more like a place of worship."

Cade glanced at the cybo. "You're learning."

The blonde used an entry code to open the gleaming steel grille and led them into the vault. She spoke to the security droid on duty and followed it down to the box depository. She returned a couple of minutes later. The droid was behind her, carrying the long safe-deposit box, which it placed on the table in front of Cade and Janek. The blonde tapped in the two sets of code numbers, then stepped back.

"All yours, Marshal Cade," she said, and left.

Cade raised the lid of the box.

At first it appeared that the box contained nothing but money. In neat, banded blocks of thousand-dollar bills.

"Looks like Culver was saving for old age," Cade said, lifting out stacks of the bills.

"He must have started saving the day he left kinder-garten, then," Janek remarked.

Cade removed the last of the cash. On the bottom of the box was a thin, square card packet. Inside was a computer disk.

"The jackpot, partner," Cade said. He handed the disk to Janek. "Look after this."

"What about the money?" Janek asked out of sheer curiosity.

Cade looked at him, his face deadpan. "You want it?"

"Not funny, Thomas," the cybo chided.

Cade dumped the money back in the deposit box and closed the lid. He signaled to the waiting security droid.

"You can put it back now."

They made their way out of the bank, and Cade went over to have a word with the local police. Then he flung himself back behind the wheel and drove out of Sag Harbor, picking up the route that would return them to New York.

Janek showed his usual interest in the surroundings, his eyes taking in everything they were passing. His thirst for knowledge seemed endless, and his curiosity was never stifled.

"That helicopter we tangled with," he remarked after about a quarter of an hour.

"What about it?" Cade asked.

"It's back," Janek said.

He said it low key, with no sense of urgency in his voice, and for a second Cade failed to comprehend, but only until the helicopter swooped into view, swaying as it hovered above the expressway directly ahead of their speeding cruiser.

"Shit!" Cade yelled, yanking the wheel hard to the left.

The cruiser lurched, tires squealing under the pressure of the extreme maneuver. Cade hauled the wheel around in the opposite direction, bringing the car back in line.

Janek had grabbed the SPAS and slipped off the safety. He powered down his window, setting himself to stand off any attack from the menacing helicopter.

The chopper curved around to hang ahead of them again. The side hatch was open, and the ugly snout of a heavy, rapid-fire autocannon jutted out from the chopper's cabin.

The cannon opened up, and a stream of 30 mm high-velocity shells hammered at the Ford. The expressway blew chunks of asphalt into the air. Cade swerved violently. He pulled the car away from the main stream of cannon fire but failed to clear it completely. Shells chewed at the right front fender, filling the air with shards of metal, but the tire wasn't touched. The fire-spitting helicopter overflew the hurtling car, giving Cade breathing space in which to increase his already breakneck speed.

"Dammit, Janek, we're sitting ducks."

"Then let's get the hell out of it."

Even as Cade stepped on the brake, sending the cruiser into a rubber-burning slide, the helicopter hit them again.

This time it came diving in at their rear, raking the cruiser with shell fire. The rear window blew out, and the 30 mm slugs ripped into bodywork and upholstery. One of the rear tires exploded with a heavy thump, and the slewing car began to bounce heavily.

Cade wrestled with the wheel, aware that he was losing the battle. The cruiser arced around suddenly, slamming into the crash barrier at the side of the expressway. It slithered along the metal rail, while Cade kept hitting the brake. Finally he brought the car to a wrenching, shuddering halt. He kicked open his door and rolled out onto the highway with Janek close behind him, still clutching the SPAS.

Snatching his .357 from its holster, Cade circled the front of the wrecked car and vaulted the crash barrier, throwing himself into the field of grass and shrubbery that lay on the far side. As he thrust his way through, he could hear Janek pounding along behind him, and over all other sounds the thwack of the chopper's rotors as it searched for them.

As Cade pushed deeper into the undergrowth, he picked up the sound of distant voices and, throwing a backward glance, he saw armed figures clearing the crash barrier.

The chopper had called in reinforcements.

5

The rattle of an autoweapon reached Cade's ears. He heard the passing bullets tear at the undergrowth. The Justice cop felt his anger rising. He hated being shot at, but even more he hated the thought of running.

He hauled himself to a stop and turned, the .357 swinging up in his fist. He spotted the dark-clad figures coming at him through the tall grasses. He cupped his left hand under his right, bracing the Magnum. His finger squeezed back on the trigger. The powerful handgun rocked in his fist.

One of the pursuing gunmen twisted out of control and crashed hard down on the ground. He was out of the running, and close by, the heavy boom of the SPAS told Cade his partner had joined in the fight. Janek began to fire in a steady routine, taking out two more of the attackers before the remainder turned in hasty retreat.

"Let's go," Cade suggested, and the pair moved off, heading for a stand of timber in the near distance.

Overhead the dark shape of the helicopter monitored their movements. Without warning, it dropped, sweeping low across the grassy meadow. The tall grasses rippled like waves on the ocean beneath the rotor wash.

The chopper roared in toward them, the sound of its motor rising to a loud howl of fury, but its 30 mm cannon was unable to fire on them during forward flight.

Janek faced the oncoming craft, the SPAS to his shoulder. He led the advancing machine, then trig-

gered a couple of loads at the canopy. The shot struck
the lower nose of the chopper as it flew by them. The
side gunner swung his weapon around and loosed off a
number of shots in passing that went wide of the mark.

"Those trees," Cade yelled. "They'll give us some
cover."

He began to sprint toward the stand of timber. Janek followed, scanning the area.

The group of gunmen appeared again, off to the left.
They'd stayed under cover until they were level with
Cade and Janek, and now they were making another
attack.

At the same time the chopper dropped out of the sky,
almost reaching ground level as it skimmed along, Janek turned, aware of its closeness. He swung the shotgun, attempting to fire, but the pilot increased his
speed.

Janek tried to turn aside, his powerful legs driving
him forward. Then the chopper's landing skid caught
him in the lower back. The cybo felt himself lifted and
thrown through the air. He lost his grip on the SPAS.
The earth rushed up to meet him, and he crashed to the
ground. His senses went all to hell, and the day went
blank on him.

Cade had witnessed his partner's knockdown. He
forgot about his own safety and turned to face the advancing gunmen.

The helicopter edged in his direction and settled to the
ground, and the muzzle of the 30 mm cannon arced
around to cover him. A dark-clad figure moved up beside the gunner. Cade recognized him.

It was the man he'd seen talking to Barney Culver in
the warehouse.

The man who had arranged Culver's death.

The merc called Tane.

"Just put the gun down, Marshal Cade. You don't stand a chance."

Cade eyed the encircling gunmen. He tossed his gun to the ground.

"Get on board," Tane said.

Cade climbed in through the open hatch under Tane's watchful eye and gun.

One of the gunmen called to Tane. "What about the cybo?"

"You deal with it," Tane said. To the chopper pilot he said, "Get us out of here."

The chopper climbed, then swung around and headed in the general direction of New York.

"GREAT," said the merc who had asked the question about Janek. "We get to dump the tinman."

He glanced at his two partners.

"How do you dump a cyborg?"

One of them shrugged, eyeing Janek's motionless form.

"Unscrew his arms and legs?"

"Grab hold and let's get him in the trunk of the car before we get sightseers."

The trio slung their autoweapons over their shoulders, then bent over Janek, reaching for his limbs.

The cybo burst into movement without warning.

His right arm swept up and around, the edge of his hand crunching against the closest nose, crushing the bone and snapping the man's head back. He fell over backward, clapping his hands to his bloody face.

Janek's left hand closed over the second merc's wrist as he rose to his feet. The merc tried to break free, but Janek's grip was unrelenting. Janek turned the arm against the joint, lifting and raising the moaning man up on his toes. He curled his right arm around the neck, pulled him close and twisted. The neck snapped with a brittle sound, and the merc became a dead weight in the cyborg's arm. Janek let him fall as he turned to meet the remaining merc.

This one had managed to free his autoweapon. He made a desperate attempt to level it at Janek, but the cyborg slapped it aside with an easy punch. The man panicked, his finger jerking back on the trigger. The sound of the firing weapon was the last thing he heard before Janek stepped in close and snapped his neck with a savage twist of his hands.

Janek turned to the first merc he'd hit. The man was crawling about on hands and knees, moaning in agony. Blood dribbled in glistening strings from his nose and mouth. Bending over, Janek hauled him to this feet. As he pulled the man upright, the merc lashed out with his right fist. The blow struck Janek across the jaw. He didn't even flinch but just stared at the merc.

"Wasting your time. It would be wiser if you answered some questions."

"No way," the merc spit through bloody lips. He dropped a hand to the small of his back and yanked a hideaway gun from a concealed holster. He jammed the barrel up at Janek's face, his fingers easing back on the trigger.

"Awkward son of a bitch," Janek said.

His fingers clamped around the barrel of the hideaway, twisting it savagely. The merc howled in pain as two of his fingers were broken in the process.

"We could do this all day," Janek said. "Make it easy on yourself."

The merc relaxed, apparently accepting his position. Janek let him have a little slack.

Without warning, the merc dropped to his knees, scooping up one of the SMGs dropped by his dead companions. His finger curled around the trigger, and he angled the weapon up at Janek's towering form. The autoweapon crackled loudly, but the volley of slugs struck empty air.

Janek had gone to ground in a long, low dive, his fingers reaching for the SPAS. He caught hold of the combat shotgun and pulled it to him as he rolled, turning his body in toward the cursing merc. This time the cyborg didn't hesitate. He triggered twice, blowing sizable holes through his opponent's upper body. The merc gave a stunned grunt, flopping back, his arms flung wide in death.

As the echo of the shots died away, Janek lay staring at the dead merc. He shook his head, angry at his over-reaction. He should have applied his inbuilt logic and gone for a wounding shot, rather than blowing the merc away. Killing the merc had erased any chance of finding out where Cade had been taken. Janek stood up, lost for the moment. He was inwardly cursing his stupidity. He knew that this wasn't supposed to happen to him. He was supposed to act rationally, but somehow he'd allowed his feelings to affect his actions. Because of that, he had lost a possible source of information.

Janek headed back to the highway. There was a black Dodge Laser-Six parked just behind the wrecked cruiser. He climbed in and fired the powerful engine. He knocked it into gear and took off with a screech of tires.

He needed to get back to the city and his computer. The disk in his pocket might hold information that could lead him to the place where Cade was being taken. It was a long shot, but it was all Janek had now.

WHEN HE EMERGED from the Midtown tunnel, he abruptly pulled the car over and brought it to a stop by the sidewalk. He climbed out, went to a pay phone and called the department. He wasn't sure what had prompted him.

Braddock's face swam into view on the vid-screen.

"Don't talk, just listen," Braddock said. "I've been hanging around waiting for one of you to call. All kinds of stuff is going down here. I've even had Police Chief Norris ordering you off. Now I don't know what you and Cade have dug up, but there's been some kind of panic. Just stay low for a while, okay? Do what you have to but stay loose. Don't come near the department. I'll cover for you guys the best I can, Janek."

The line went dead. Janek stared at the screen. He was glad he'd called in before showing himself. It must have been intuition, as Cade called it—a feeling that warned of possible danger. Janek was curious about how he, a cyborg, had developed such a sense. When he had the time, he would sit down and analyze it.

Right now he had to stay out of sight as much as possible. But he needed a safe base, someplace where he could take a look at the computer disk they had found in Culver's safe-deposit box. He returned to the car and on impulse drove across town to Kate Bannion's apartment block. He didn't know if she would be in or not. He parked in the basement and left the Dodge in a dark corner.

As he crossed the parking area, he spotted Kate's car in its usual slot. He took the elevator to her floor. He checked the corridor before he walked to her door and pressed the buzzer on the door-vid.

"Janek," he said.

Kate opened up and let him in, glancing over his shoulder.

"Where's T.J.?"

Janek filled her in on recent events, bringing her up to date with his call to Braddock.

"What have you guys uncovered?"

Janek's lopsided shrug gave her the answer. "I need to access your computer, Kate," he said.

She gave a wry grin. "That's a new way of saying it," she murmured.

Janek's puzzled expression made her smile even more. "Forget it, Janek." She indicated the computer on the desk at one end of the room. "Help yourself."

Janek switched on and slid the disk into the drive. He watched the screen intently, nodding to himself as text appeared.

"Is it what you expected?" Kate asked, peering over Janek's shoulder.

"Give me a minute and I'll be able to tell you."

Janek scrolled through the information on the monitor. The text consisted mainly of names, and in addition, what looked to be a number of locations.

"Placid Base?" Kate read. "Where's that? I've never heard of it."

"It's a military establishment," Janek said. "At least it's tying in with the other military references we've been picking up."

"Munro. Poole. Both colonels, one Army, the other Air Force?"

Janek said, "And there's a familiar name. Lukas Tane. That's the name of the guy T.J. heard talking to Culver at the warehouse."

"You could run a check on the names," Kate suggested.

"I would never have thought of doing that," the cyborg remarked sarcastically.

Kate punched him on the shoulder. "Watch it, smartass."

"Recognize those names?" Janek asked.

Kate stared at the screen.

"Yes. The three dead Amosin employees."

"No wonder Culver panicked when George Takagi dug them out of the data bank."

"He already knew the background."

"Exactly."

At the end of the text was a single, incomplete sentence, underlined for emphasis: "August 18: Skylance."

"That's the day after tomorrow," Kate said. "And what is Skylance?"

Janek cleared the screen and began to tap in the access code that would link him with the computer in his office at the department. The moment the confirmation code blinked on the monitor, he gave the command for the computer to transmit the information he'd been gathering.

"Before we left the office, I set the computer on a deep search. T.J. wanted information on the combat droids that killed Takagi. I had to break into ComNet, the military computer system. Highly illegal, but you know how it is when T.J. gets on a roll."

He sat and watched the screen text. It flashed and changed, scrolling long code lists before it settled and

Janek's own code reference indicated that his questions were about to be answered.

"The ID numbers I got from the combat droids indicate they are listed as surplus items, taken out of commission over three years ago. They're supposed to be in a reserve storage facility at the Amosin Corporation's robotics division. No indication that the storage has been canceled."

"So they were being used illegally," Kate said.

Janek fed in the most recent information he'd gathered. The data banks came up with the answers within a couple of minutes.

The weapons found in the warehouse should have been stored in an armory upstate. According to the computer, they were still there.

"Someone is building himself quite an arsenal," Janek murmured as he studied the text on the screen. "Let's see what we can find out about our two colonels and friend Tane."

Colonel Clayton Munro and Colonel Edwin Poole were both senior officers in U.S. High Command, Eastern Division. Their ranks gave them wide-ranging power and influence. The list of credentials on their service records were impressive. Both men were lifers who had earned their positions through long service and by distinguishing themselves as good soldiers.

Lukas Tane was an ex-soldier. He'd served in Special Forces in most of the world's trouble spots. He had left the Army two years previously. During his service, he had operated in a special unit run by Clayton Munro. After leaving the Army, Tane had formed his own mercenary unit, consisting of himself and ex-members of his Special Forces unit.

Finally Janek asked about Skylance.

Skylance: Orbiting weapons satellite platform. Integrated laser and missile systems. Under the control of U.S. Military Command. Manned by permanent complement of six-man crew plus six androids. Skylance's potential as a defensive weapon is difficult to qualify due to the destructive enormity of the armaments it possesses. A conservative estimate allows for the possibility of Skylance being capable of laying down a threat to any nation on Earth and carrying that threat through. Skylance is protected by the most sophisticated defense system in operation. Hunter-killer satellites ring Skylance and are capable of detecting and destroying any attack, whether it comes from earth or even space itself...

Janek canceled the text and leaned back in his seat. He glanced at Kate. "Now we know what Skylance is," he said.

"Oh boy," she breathed. "But what the hell has all this to do with three dead Amosin employees and all the other stuff that's been going on?"

"I can only think of one word," Janek said. "Conspiracy."

"Against what? And who?"

Janek raised his hands. "Take your pick. A potential enemy. The U.S. government. Maybe a military coup."

Kate began to pace the room, her eyes searching the walls as if she expected the answer to come leaping out at her. She ran a hand through her red hair in frustration.

"This is crazy, Janek. What can we do?"

"*We?*"

"Yes, dammit. If you think I'm sitting at home like the little woman, then you're in for a hell of a shock. T.J. is out there somewhere. He could be hurt or worse, and he'll need our help. I won't sit by and desert him. So get used to the idea—partner."

Janek smiled. One thing he had picked up from Cade was to accept that it was useless to argue when a woman made up her mind. It was no good fighting it.

"Something I almost forgot," he said, and faced the computer again. He keyed in a request for information on Placid Base.

The answer came slowly, the computer having to search deep and hard.

"Placid Base," Janek read. "Decommissioned six years ago and abandoned by the military. It was a training camp for Special Forces. Located near Lake Placid in the Adirondack Mountains. That area took some heavy hits during the chem war. It became uninhabitable. The military even pulled out eventually due to the breakdown of the area and the fact that it became a haven for mutants."

"If we do have some kind of conspiracy," Kate said, "there'd be a need for a base. Somewhere for them to operate out of. I can't think of a better place—right out in the badlands, no one around for miles."

"Except the mutants," Janek told her.

Kate shuddered. "Don't remind me."

"Having second thoughts about joining the team?"

Kate waved a finger under his nose. "No, you don't, Janek. I'm not quitting, so don't try and scare me off."

"Would I?"

"You work with T. J. Cade, don't you?"

Janek nodded.

"I rest my case."

Switching off the computer, Janek ejected the disk and slipped it into his pocket. Even if the disk was taken from him, he wouldn't lose the information. The cyborg had committed it all to his own memory banks.

"So where are we going?" Kate asked.

"We'll start with Placid Base. First I need to get my hands on some weapons. No point going in empty-handed."

"Give me a couple of minutes to get changed," Kate said.

Janek picked up the phone and punched in a number. He watched the vid-screen fuzz into life. A lean, hard-eyed face appeared.

"Eddie," Janek said in greeting.

"Hey, Janek, it's been a long time."

"I need a favor, Eddie. How soon can you open the store?"

Eddie Culchek stared at the cybo. "You serious?"

"I don't have time for joking right now, Eddie."

"Okay, pal, come around."

"My credit good, Eddie?"

Eddie grinned nervously. "Sure, Janek. You and T.J. always did right by me. I owe you guys."

"I'll be there," Janek said, and broke the connection.

Kate emerged from the bedroom. She had changed into a one-piece jumpsuit and lace-up boots.

"Ready when you are," she said.

Janek ignored her, and he looked toward the door intently. "Janek?" Kate asked. "What—?"

There was a heavy crash of sound, and the apartment door blew inward across the room. Janek reached out to grab Kate, pulling her tight against him to shield her from flying debris.

The rush of heavy footsteps filled the room.

Janek shoved Kate behind him and turned, his hand snaking the autopistol from its holster.

He saw three armed figures crowding into the room. They wore dark combat suits and carried autorifles.

Two were droids. Janek recognized the hard, angular features the instant he tracked in with the pistol. He triggered a pair of shots that cored through the lead droid's left eye into the brain. The droid swung around, out of control, its autorifle blasting shots into the ceiling.

Janek had changed position. He heard the angry rattle of the autorifles, heard the explosion of sound as the computer erupted. He hit the floor and rolled, feeling slivers of wood strike his legs. As he gathered his feet under him, Janek saw the second combat droid closing in. The Justice cop swept his gun around, firing quickly. The slug hit the droid's arm, jerking it off balance. The rifle sagged for a second, giving Janek the opportunity to lash out with his right foot. The blow caught the droid on the left hip, and it stumbled under the impact. Janek powered to his feet, reached the droid in a single stride and, before the droid could react, Janek caught hold and lifted it off the floor. He swung around, hurling the droid bodily across the room. The moving body collided with the third member of the strike team, the merc in charge. They went down in a struggling heap, the droid rolling free. But now Janek was following up, closing in fast. He jammed his left foot across the merc's neck, twisting it sharply. The neck snapped with a grinding crunch. He twitched violently, then lay still. In the same movement Janek grabbed the rising droid by the neck and shoulder, swung it around and shoved it through the apartment window. The eruption of glass was followed by the droid's twisting form as it vanished from sight to hurtle to the street below.

"Come on, Kate. Let's go," Janek said.

He caught hold of her hand, pulling her with him out the damaged door and along the passage to the elevator, ignoring her protests about her apartment.

Janek led the way down to the basement. He made Kate wait by the elevator while he checked the area, then took her to the Dodge. He pushed her into the passenger seat. Firing up the motor, he rolled out of the garage and swung onto the street. He gunned the motor, heading for the intersection at the front of the building. They had almost reached it when a lurching figure burst from the shadows and planted itself in their path.

Kate gave a startled yell as she recognized the battered figure of the combat droid Janek had thrown from her window.

"Even they can't be that tough," she said.

"Let's see," Janek replied grimly, jamming his foot hard down on the gas pedal.

The combat droid stood its ground, eyes gleaming with a dull red glow, arms extended.

Janek gripped the wheel so tightly the plastic began to groan under the pressure. As the howl of the engine increased, Janek let go with a yell of frustration.

The car shuddered as the point of the hood caught the combat droid in its midsection. For a few seconds it remained there, staring at Janek through the windshield, arms reaching out across the hood, then it sagged forward slowly, sliding across the hood. It arched up in the air, twisting wildly, then vanished over the roof of the car.

Turning in her seat, Kate saw it crash down on the street, bouncing and rolling across the surface, trailing a shower of sparks behind it. She was sure she could see bits and pieces flying off the body as it cartwheeled along the street. As Janek took the car around the corner, the droid vanished from sight.

"Friendly sort of guy, wasn't he?" Janek said airily. "The way he just dropped in to visit."

Kate's disapproving glare silenced him, and he concentrated on driving.

The day was slipping away quickly. The heavy ball of the sun was sinking behind the city's tall silhouette, leaving the sky deep and sullen. The heat lingered, persistent, shrouding everything. Janek eased into the traffic, heading for the Brooklyn Bridge. Once they made it across the bridge, he swung under the Queens Expressway and followed the potholed, wreck-littered feeder road that angled in toward the decaying area of the old Brooklyn Navy Yard.

The long-abandoned shipyard had changed hands a number of times over the years. Street gangs had laid claim to it during the first quarter of the century as Brooklyn went into a long decline. The sprawling borough had seen a massive influx of people seeking protection from the violence and crime sweeping the suburbs of the city. Overcrowding and poor amenities had only added to Brooklyn's problems. Yet despite the social difficulties, Brooklyn survived, as it always had. Even the darkest times had failed to extinguish its spirit. The famed resilience of the area had seen her through; hard times were borne with stoic optimism, and Brooklyn had asserted itself over the next few decades. Always able to handle its own affairs, the borough had

faced the hazards of the new century, survived and
forged its own unique place.

The gangs who had taken over the Navy yard were
forced out by the vigilante groups who had decided
enough was enough. Pitched battles had raged for over
six months, and dozens were killed on both sides. The
gangs were finally defeated, and the Navy yard was left
empty and gutted. It had stayed that way for almost ten
years. Then there began to emerge a new breed of in-
habitant of the complex. The Navy yard became the
focal point for the traveling groups of traders who
moved back and forth across the continent. These itin-
erants, in their mobile caravans, were the purveyors of
black market goods. If it couldn't be obtained anywhere else, you went to the Brooklyn Yards, as the new
venue became known. Some traders established permanent warehouses, becoming brokers who handled
goods, bartered and stored for all the others. The law-
enforcement agencies tolerated the traders. They had to.
The public would have lynched anyone who tried to
close them down. In many cases the traders were the
only source for certain goods, and everyone sought
them out.

Eddie Culchek was one of those traders. He handled
anything that would turn a profit—and one of Eddie's
specialties was weapons. It was said that Eddie could get
you anything if you were prepared to pay for it. Eddie
himself would never acknowledge that statement to
anyone face-to-face, but it was well known that he had
never once failed to satisfy his customers.

Darkness was falling by the time Janek rolled the
Dodge into the Brooklyn Yards. Powerful floodlights,
powered by generators, lit the crowded area. It had the
atmosphere of a carnival. Street entertainers played to

the crowds. Music blared from mobile speakers. The rich odors of ethnic foods wafted and mingled in the air. There were stalls selling fresh vegetables from the Midwest, brought in by fast jets. Refrigerated trailers hauled in meat from the independent ranchers and other trucks delivered electronic goods from the California factories. There was even a brisk trade in service droids.

"Janek, I didn't realize what went on over here," Kate said. "Is it always like this?"

"The traders provide what the people want," Janek said. "Supply and demand. It's the American way, isn't it, Kate?"

He drove through the crowded area, turning in alongside a warehouse edging the murky waters of the East River. As Janek brought the vehicle to a stop, a pair of armed men slipped from the shadows and stood on either side of the car, their autoweapons aimed at the cyborg. Janek climbed out, his hands held well away from his body.

"Easy, guys," he said. "I'm here to see Eddie."

"That you, Janek?" came a voice from the shadows.

"Eddie, you've been watching too many TV cop shows."

Eddie Culchek came to stand in the glare of the headlights. He was a slim, dark man dressed in a bright shirt and black pants. He wore a silk bandanna around his neck. It wasn't there for effect. It concealed a wide, nasty-looking scar—a reminder of his earlier, tougher days.

"TV cop shows are my favorites." He grinned. "Hey, you look like you been through hard times, Janek." Eddie flicked a finger over the dark bloodstains on Janek's clothing.

"It doesn't get any easier," Janek said. "Eddie, I need the merchandise fast. No time for the jazz tonight."

"You need help? Take the boys if you do."

"Thanks, but this is something I have to handle on my own."

"Whatever you say." Culchek eyed the Dodge. "Laser-Six. Nice wheels, Janek. They must look after you Justice boys."

"Nothing to do with the department, actually," Janek said, sensing Culchek's interest. "It's what they call liberated. From undesirables. Mine to do what I want."

"That so? Maybe we could work something out. You need anything extra...something special?"

"Could be," the cyborg said. "I do need to borrow something different."

"How different?"

"Something fast. Silent. Like a helicopter, Eddie."

Culchek grinned. "I like your style. You always think big. Come on inside, and we'll see what we can figure out for you."

"Be back soon," Janek said to Kate, and followed Eddie inside the cavernous, decaying warehouse.

Watching him go, Kate sank back in the comfortable seat and allowed her thoughts to wander. They didn't take long to define themselves because there was only one thing on Kate's mind.

Cade.

His whereabouts.

And more importantly, his state of health.

6

The overpowering stench reaching in through the very walls of his cell told Cade he was in the Chemlands. That was basic information. It didn't tell him *which* contaminated area of the American continent he was in.

The legacy of the war between the U.S. and the Islamic Federation was a number of chemically ruined tracts of land. Anywhere a biological missile had landed, it had spread its malignant cargo of mutated spores. These powerful strains had the ability to multiply and breed and develop new mutations. They were developed to lay waste areas of fertile land, producing enzymes that were virtually indestructible. Secondary missiles contained spores that attacked the human animal, creating mutations that would take generations to breed out of the system. It was only due to errors in the Islamic Federation's guidance systems that the missiles failed to hit their primary targets—major U.S. food-growing areas. The bulk of the missiles landed in rural areas, away from the great wheat fields and stock ranches. A number got through and lay waste to valuable tracts of land. The missiles aimed at U.S. areas of high population densities overshot every target. But the chemicals distributed infected enough people to create a great number of mutations.

Cade had seen firsthand the results of the missile strikes, and the memories had stayed with him for a long time. They were things he didn't want to have to see again. Even though the visual memories faded with time, Cade never forgot the smell that greeted him when his Marine unit had entered one of the infected areas. The stench had reminded him of death and decay. It was a rancid, cloying scent that seemed to penetrate through clothing and into the very pores of the skin.

It was the same stench he was breathing in now.

The room he'd been thrown into some hours back was small and basic, constructed from prefabricated concrete. The design and layout told him one more thing.

He was on a military base. There was something about the design and feel of military buildings that was unlike anything else. Cade had seen enough of them during his hitch with the Marines, and he wasn't likely to forget. Military bases were the same, no matter where they were situated, on earth or an asteroid colony. A military base just couldn't be disguised as anything else.

The moment the helicopter had lifted off, Tane had ordered Cade blindfolded. He had been pushed to the rear of the cabin, away from any viewports, and that was where he'd remained during the flight. It had been a long one. By the time touchdown had been made, darkness had already fallen. Cade had been dragged across the landing area and into a building where his cell had been waiting.

The room contained a metal-frame cot covered by a thin mattress. There was a single chair and table. A recessed light, covered by reinforced glass, provided illumination. There was nothing else. Just the gray, cold walls and a barred window.

And the penetrating stench of the Chemlands.

Cade stood at the barred window, staring out across the darkened compound. There were no exterior lights showing. He could make out the perimeter fence. High, steel linked, with tall pylons every so often, topped by inactive floodlights. Beyond the fence lay the twisted shape of the forest, trees and undergrowth radically altered by the effects of the chemical attack. He wondered idly if there were any of the mutated survivors out there. Maybe watching the camp themselves. Not that it made any difference. The mutants had no time for normal people. They held society as a whole responsible for what had happened to *them*. Cade couldn't rely on help from the mutants.

He heard the electric bolts slam back as someone activated the door mechanism. Cade turned to inspect his visitors.

Lukas Tane was the first to enter. The mercenary leader was clad in a black jumpsuit, with a shoulder rig carrying a large Beretta autopistol. He was a tall man, strongly built without looking bulky. His lean, tanned face was slightly marred by a couple of small scars along the left cheek and jawline, which lent him a dangerous look. He stepped to the side of the cell to allow his two companions to crowd in behind him.

They were clearly related. Their similar genes showed in the heavy-boned facial resemblance. They had the same small, bitter eyes, almost reptilian in their cold regard for the world around them. They stared at Cade with open hostility. Both were armed, carrying autopistols similar to Tane's, though they wore them in high-ride holsters on their right hips.

"I have to admire you, Cade," Lukas Tane said. "One man causing us all this shit."

He moved away from the wall to the center of the cell, watching Cade all the time. The merc seemed faintly amused by the whole proceedings.

"I don't have the time to dance around with this," he explained. "Too many things about to happen. So let me spell it out for you.

"Personally I don't give a damn whether you cooperate or not. This thing is too big for one man to stop. I'd off you right now if I had my way. But you've got the top brass worried in case there's been a major leak. All I see is a cop who got in over his head, figuring he'd struck lucky. Truth is, Cade, you ain't got a damn thing, and I figure to bury you along with that."

"You finished?" Cade asked. Cade knew he was in danger, but he wasn't terribly shaken by Tane's hard act—though he had to accept the man had all the cards. "Just what do you expect me to say?"

"What did you find on Barney Culver's boat?"

"Culver—dead. But you already know that."

"You were on that boat a damn long time after you got it back to the quayside."

"Police procedure's as slow as it ever was."

Tane's face suddenly hardened. "Cut the crap, Cade. You find any kind of information on the boat?"

"Nothing."

"The bastard's lying, Lukas," one of the other men said. "Ask him what he did in the goddamn bank."

"Opened a savings account for my retirement," Cade said.

"Son of a bitch," the man snarled, lunging forward.

Cade remained where he was, having little space to retreat. It looked as though he wasn't going to offer any resistance. In fact, he held off until the merc was close enough so he could smell the man's stale breath. Only then did the Justice cop move, turning slightly and bringing his right arm up in a slashing sweep that struck the man across the throat. The force of the blow lifted the man off his feet, tossing him backward at the same time. He crashed to the floor of the cell, gagging heavily, his beefy face darkening as he struggled for breath.

The third man snatched his pistol from its holster, swinging it around to cover Cade. Tane leaned forward and pushed the gun aside.

"Back off, Hog," he advised. "Help your brother up. I'll keep Cade under control."

Tane slipped his Beretta from its holster and aimed it at Cade.

"This isn't getting us anywhere, Cade."

Cade failed to hold back the grin that curled his lips.

"You mean I should have let him hit me?"

Tane's eyes lost their good humor. The muscles in his jaw tightened, and without warning he slashed the heavy autopistol across the side of Cade's head. The sharp impact turned Cade sideways. He felt the hot rush of blood down the side of his face.

"Yeah, gimme the bastard..." someone snarled.

Out of the haze that was fogging Cade's vision he saw a broad figure lunging at him. He tried to pull aside but failed. The heavy bulk slammed into him, knocking him back against the wall. The impact drove the breath from Cade's lungs, and before he could recover, a huge fist struck his jaw, spinning him off balance. Spitting blood, Cade threw up his arms to ward off further blows, but they were knocked aside. He felt blow after blow banging into his face and body. The initial pain quickly receded, the blows becoming a numbing succession of thumps. Cade didn't even notice he'd fallen until someone started kicking him in the ribs.

Dimly he could hear raised voices. The kicking stopped, and Cade was pulled roughly to his feet, pushed back against the wall.

"See what happens when you get mouthy?"

Cade cracked a painful eye and stared into Lukas Tane's angry face.

"Tane, your hospitality sucks," he mumbled through bloody, split lips.

"This the best you can do, Lukas?" someone asked.

"Boys got carried away a little, Colonel," Tane said.

Cade blinked, trying to clear his vision. He wanted to see the man standing just behind Tane, but try as he might, his eyes kept blurring. All he could make out was a tall figure in a uniform, insignia glittering under the light. He shook his head in frustration.

"Give him a break, Lukas," the voice commanded. *Command* was exactly the word. The man didn't ask. His manner was taut, full of authority, and Tane responded to it instantly.

"Yes, sir. Outside, you two."

As they all trooped from the cell, Cade caught the colonel's final words.

"Lukas, before you kill this man, I want to know everything he's found out about us. We can't afford to miss a damn thing. Dammit, man, I won't allow the fate of this country to be jeopardized by some stupid cop!"

The door banged shut, bolts sliding into their chambers with oiled finality.

Cade dragged himself to the cot and fell across it. He managed to roll on his back. Lying there, staring up at the ceiling through his blurred eyes, he allowed his mind to go over what he'd heard and tried to make some kind of sense out of it. He failed, because his thoughts refused to gel. The beating he'd received had left him unable to think cohesively. He needed time to get his head in order—if they allowed him that luxury. The problem was he didn't think they would. When they finally did decide he had outlived his usefulness, he'd be a dead man.

7

The sleek, matt black helicopter dropped silently out of the night sky, angling in the direction of a tangled mass of undergrowth. The twisted growth lay against the upper slope of a timbered knoll with a level top. Janek had decided this would provide the most accessible landing place for his strike against the military base.

Strapped in the passenger seat beside Janek, Kate Bannion stared into the blackness below. As far as she was concerned, they could have been dropping into hell itself. There was nothing to indicate how far off the ground they might be or where they actually were. The night was darker than any she'd ever lived through.

Easing the stick, Janek worked the foot controls, bringing the chopper down in a perfectly executed landing. He made touchdown with barely a bump. The cyborg's intricate optical system contained a microchip-controlled night-vision capability. The dense night opened up before his eyes, bathed in a soft green light.

As the helicopter settled, Janek cut the already silenced motor. The rotors began to slow as he shut down the craft's power.

Swiveling his seat, Janek bent over the large holdall he'd brought with him from Eddie Culchek's. He was already suited up for the night's activity in a black bodysuit and combat boots. He opened the straps fastening the holdall and exposed the armaments stored inside. Kate watched in fascination as Janek pulled out a combat rifle fitted with a laser sight. He picked up a full magazine of hollowpoint slugs that had a second magazine taped to it for quick reloading. Janek locked the magazine in place, snapping back the cocking bolt. He leaned the rifle against the bulkhead, then reached into the depths of the bag for a belt hung with pouches. In the pouches were extra magazines for the rifle, a sound suppressor and a number of grenades. He clipped the belt around his waist. Slipping his autopistol from the shoulder rig, Janek checked that it was fully loaded.

"That'll have to be it," he said. "No time for anything too fancy this trip."

He produced a tube holding camouflage cosmetic and smeared it on his face and hands. His final move was to pick up a dark baseball cap and pull it on over his white-blond hair.

"Well?" he asked.

Kate nodded. "I'd never see you in the dark."

"If I do find T.J. in there and get him out," Janek said, "he's going to give me hell."

"For letting me come along? I'll handle that," she said. "Janek, I feel safer out here than I would have in New York."

"Okay. Now listen. You know how to use the radio if you have to call for help... but only as a last resort. Calling outside help could be risky the way things are shaping up at the moment."

"I understand. Don't worry, I won't push the panic button."

"You have the SMG I gave you?"

Kate held it up. "Don't worry about me. I'll keep anyone away from the helicopter."

"We might need to get off in a hurry," Janek said. "And remember, once I get near, I'll hit the signal device I'm carrying. It will activate the panel light I showed you."

"Soon as I see that, I fire up the motor and boost the power like you explained."

Janek glanced at his watch. "It should take me about an hour to reach the base. Allow another thirty minutes to check the place out. If I'm right and they have T.J., I'll make it short and sharp. I don't know about return time. We might have company, so that part we play by ear."

"It will be getting light by then," Kate pointed out.

"Don't remind me. Nothing we can do about that."

"Janek, do you think he'll be there?"

The cyborg stared at her, his eyes unblinking, studying her beautiful face. He realized it was an odd time to be experiencing the realization, but he was suddenly aware why T.J. had such strong feelings for this woman. Although she was a wonderful person, her appearance expressed an elusive, compelling inner quality. She was lovely, and for the first time he understood that the human appreciation for beauty was an amazing facility.

His attention snapped back to the matter at hand, and he gave her an embarrassed grin before answering. "I hope so, Kate. The odds would seem to be in my favor. If they'd only wanted to kill T.J., they could have done it when they captured him. They didn't, so it must mean they need to talk with him. Probably to try and get information from him. Safer for them to do that in an isolated place, where they're unlikely to be disturbed. This base has something to do with their scheme, so we have a reasonable chance T.J. is here."

"Find him, Janek. And bring both of you back."

The cyborg nodded. He opened the side hatch and slipped out into the night. Kate closed the hatch, hearing the electro-bolts snap into place. Janek had already vanished from sight, merging with the darkness. Kate leaned forward and touched the button that blacked out the canopy, then sat back to wait. The first few minutes already seemed like an eternity to her. . . .

JANEK WORKED his way down the uneven slope, his quick responses enabling him to anticipate the difficult areas ahead of him. He held the combat rifle across his chest, his finger resting on the guard beside the trigger. The cyborg's night vision allowed him to move faster than any human. A couple of times he was faced by obstacles in the form of wide fissures in the earth, but he was able to leap across them, landing lightly on the far side. He was a powerful specimen who could out-perform the best athletes.

In situations like this, his inbuilt capabilities gave him a distinct advantage. Janek was able to increase the power in his limbs at will, bringing into play the full potential of the hydraulic system in his arms and legs—Janek's muscles. The compact, high-efficiency pumps were driven by electricity, derived from the plutonium heart protected by an indestructible casing. The pluto-nium pellet would keep Janek alive for an unlimited period.

Reaching the base of the slope, Janek pushed into the deep black band of the forested area between him and the base. He found himself striding through tangled, gnarled trees and undergrowth that had developed in odd shapes and sizes. The chemical poisoning had cre-ated weird, unpredictable mutated strains of the origi-nal plants. The ground underfoot was soft and spongy, thick with rotted vegetation and pools of stagnant wa-ter. There was a humid, overripe stench all around. Janek registered the odor but was able to dismiss it. Any human in the middle of the forest would have been overcome by the heavy stench of decay.

As he moved along, Janek heard strange slithering sounds coming from the depths of the undergrowth. He was aware that mutated strains of rodents and even snakes had developed out here in the Chemlands. As long as they didn't interfere with his trek, though, he wasn't going to worry. He had no reason to fear them.

Janek traversed the forest and the wild tangle of a far-reaching thicket, where the thorny branches grabbed at his clothing. His clear vision allowed him to avoid the marshy ground and the gaseous pools that were scattered throughout the area. He made his journey in less than the hour he'd predicted, and finally broke clear of the thicket and spotted the perimeter fence of the abandoned base less than eight hundred yards ahead. The terrain between the thicket and the fence had been cleared of all vegetation, leaving an exposed stretch of ground to cover.

Crouching in the shadows, the cyborg scanned the area. To his right, at the point where the western and southern sections of the perimeter fence joined, there was a watchtower, and he could discern the outline of an armed guard in the box. There was a powerful spotlight mounted on a swivel bracket, as well, ready to be turned on any unwelcome guest.

Looking beyond the fence, Janek caught a glimpse of something vaguely familiar. Resting on a concrete landing pad was a helicopter. Fine-focusing his eyes, Janek was able to pick out details of the chopper's fuselage, such as the bullet damage on its panels close to the tail rotor. The last time he'd seen that helicopter it had been lifting off with Cade on board, and previous to that it had been hovering over Barney Culver's boat off Sag Harbor.

Janek nodded to himself. His assumption had been correct. The base was far from deserted.

Janek eased the rifle off his shoulder. From one of his pockets in the combat suit he drew a long black suppressor. Swiftly he screwed it onto the threaded tip of the rifle's barrel. Activating the laser sight, Janek raised the rifle to his shoulder and laid his aim on the distant guard. The moment the red dot centered on the target's head, Janek eased back on the trigger, sending a silent bullet winging across the open space to embed itself directly between his eyes. The guard stiffened, leaned back under the impact, then slipped to the floor of the box without a sound.

Up on his feet, Janek sprinted for the watchtower, his legs driving him forward with tremendous speed. He reached the base of the tower, immediately gripped the metal support legs and scaled the fence without a moment's pause. When he reached the box, he stepped over the dead guard and climbed down the metal ladder. He stayed in the shadows, checking out the compound. The area seemed quiet, though he could see light showing from behind a number of shaded windows.

He registered the location of the helicopter again. Then he left his lookout post, and once on the ground again, moved from shadow to shadow to approach the silent machine. He crossed the final yards to where it rested on the pad. Cracking the pilot's hatch, Janek reached inside. He took a grip on the thick mass of wires under the instrument panel and ripped them free. With a satisfied smile on his face, he eased back into the darkness of the closest building.

Locating Cade was his priority. Janek used his logic to decide where his partner would be held. He was dealing with the military mind here, and whether they were honest or not made little difference. Military personnel always played the game by the rules. It was the way they were trained. From day one, the moment they donned the uniform, they were instructed to think and act in line with the military machine. Going by that, Janek figured, if they had a prisoner he would have to be held in the correct place. The guardhouse.

It took Janek no more than five minutes to locate the squat, concrete block that was the base's guardhouse. Every window had a grille of iron bars across it.

He eased around the back, flattening against the rough wall as he studied his options.

In truth they were few. Janek wasn't going to have more than one chance to get Cade out. There was no time for a fancy plan, or anything smooth and silent. This operation was going to be a simple hit-and-run deal. Once the rest of the base heard any commotion, they were going to come running.

Janek studied one of the barred windows. He slung the rifle over his shoulder, took hold of the steel grille and tested how well it was bolted into the concrete wall. Bracing himself, he planted his feet apart, pumped up his system and ripped the grille off the wall. Dropping it at his feet, he climbed up on the sill and jumped through the window.

He landed on his feet in a shower of broken glass. The room he was in held no furniture. The floor was dusty, with a few crumpled sheets of paper lying about. He crossed to the door and paused for a moment. His sensitive ears picked up the scuffle of booted feet and the murmur of voices. He also heard the rattle of weapons being cocked.

He had made his presence known and he was uninvited. There was no time—or advantage—to waiting until he was jumped on.

Janek hit the door with his shoulder, ripping it from the frame and sending it crashing into the room. He followed through, the muzzle of the combat rifle preceding him. There were three men in the room.

One raised his weapon, tracking in on Janek. The cyborg triggered on the run, and the rifle expended its volley with harsh precision. The line of slugs shredded the gunman's torso, and he went over the desk behind him in a welter of blood and scattered paperwork.

The second man, his response delayed by the fact he had to duck out of the way of the flying door, leveled his autopistol, turning his lean body in the direction of the rampaging cyborg, and triggered two fast shots. One missed completely. The second clipped the top of Janek's left shoulder, scoring the titanium casing. Janek dropped to one knee, angling the muzzle of the rifle, and touched off a blast that picked the second attacker up and hurled him into a corner of the room bloody and very dead.

The third one came at Janek from his left. He was almost too close to level his autorifle, so he swung it two-handed like a club. Janek reacted swiftly, throwing up his left arm, taking the clubbing blow across his forearm. The impact shattered the stock of the rifle. Janek followed through, the heel of his left palm slamming into the man's face and crushing his features into a bloody mask. The stunning power of the blow shoved him back across the room, and he smashed against the wall, shattering his skull. He toppled to the floor, his body thrashing in agony.

Janek stormed from the room and made his way along the starkly illuminated passage. He had a single purpose driving him—to locate and free T. J. Cade, and there wasn't a thing alive that would stop him carrying out his task.

Janek picked up the thump of boots hitting the concrete behind him. He threw himself on the ground full length a split second before the rattle of autofire filled the passage. The wall above his head exploded as a hail of high-velocity slugs pounded it. Janek felt the rattle of concrete chips bouncing off his back. He rolled over, coming to a sitting position, and his weapon found target acquisition in the shape of a combat droid.

This one, Janek realized, was a step up from the ones used in the Battery Park attack. The droid facing him now was an advanced, penetrator model, totally humanoid in design, with harsh, hostile features and extreme fighting skills.

Janek triggered the rifle, laying his volley into the droid's skull, and specifically the eyes. The projectiles ripped in and through, blowing apart the droid's electronic brain. The robot staggered, slumping against the wall before it crashed facedown on the floor. Gibberish issued from its mouth, and the hand holding the grip of the autoweapon jammed tight against the trigger, discharging the weapon's magazine into the wall.

Already on his feet and moving forward, Janek snapped in a fresh magazine and cocked the rifle. He reached the far end of the passage, but his acute hearing picked up distant voices from behind him. They were arguing, and orders were being passed back and forth. Janek pulled a grenade from his pocket, pulled the pin and tossed the spherical object back along the passage. He slipped through the end door just as the grenade detonated with a hefty explosion.

As he registered where he was, Janek saw the long, bare passage and the metal cell doors.

He also came face-to-face with a puzzled guard armed with a rifle he was already swinging into firing position. The cyborg didn't even break his stride. He backhanded the guard across the mouth, slamming him against the wall, and snatched the rifle from slack hands. Grabbing the man by the front of his fatigues, Janek lifted him off his feet to pin him against the wall. He shook him violently.

"Where's Cade? I know he's here somewhere. Give me the right answer or you're dead."

The guard, gasping for breath, waved his hands at Janek.

"Okay, okay," he whispered. "Ease up, huh? I can't fuckin' talk if I'm dead."

Janek slackened his grip, letting the man's feet touch the floor again.

The guard cleared his throat. "No sweat. He's in the third cell along the passage here."

Hauling the protesting guard behind him, Janek headed for the cell. "Unlock it," he said.

The guard shook his head. "I can't. The only guy with the code is Tane."

Still gripping the guard, Janek reached out with his right hand and took hold of the cell door's locking bar. The cyborg's fingers clamped over the bar tightly. He drew the bar out of its recess, bending it in the process. He pulled the door open and stuck his head inside.

"Is that you, T.J.?"

Cade sat up on the cot. "Took your damn time," he said through his swollen lips.

"Nag, nag, nag," Janek said. "Now let's get the hell out of here. This bunch is really inhospitable."

Cade joined him in the passage, taking the rifle Janek handed him. "Who's your friend?"

Janek glanced at the silent guard he was still holding. "Oh . . . I forgot about him."

Swinging the man through the air, Janek slammed him headfirst into the wall, then let him slump to the floor.

Just then, the passage resounded with the crackle of autofire. Bullets slammed into the walls and floor around the pair. Janek plucked another grenade from his pouch and lobbed it back along the passage. The explosion silenced the gunfire and filled the air with thick smoke. Janek slapped Cade on the shoulder.

"Let's go!" he said.

They took off at a quick pace, aware that pursuit would not be delayed for long. At the end of the passage a door blocked their way, and Janek used his shoulder to batter it open. It led to the outside.

"Follow me, T.J. I know how to get us out of here."

"You know how to stop those mothers from shooting at us?" Cade asked, falling in behind the cyborg.

"I may be good, but I'm not perfect."

They sprinted across the compound in the direction of the perimeter fence. Dawn had already started to push back the heavy blackness. The sky over the base was graying as streaks of pale light dissipated the denser shadows.

"You could have timed this better," Cade muttered.

"Sure," Janek said. "Next time I'll ask for a delay until it gets dark again. Now quit moaning and let's move."

Raised voices reached them, punctuated by gunfire that ripped into the ground around their feet.

Janek dodged between a couple of outbuildings, giving them temporary cover. The tireless cyborg maintained his pace without pause and reached the far end well ahead of Cade.

"T.J., you're out of condition."

"Yeah? You try being a punching bag for a bunch of trigger-happy mercs, then see if you fancy running a marathon."

Cade flattened against the wall of one of the buildings, the rifle trained on the far end. His instinct proved correct. A couple of the pursuing mercs appeared, their weapons probing the way ahead. Cade triggered the combat rifle, catching them before they could respond. His volley ripped into them, blowing them off their feet.

"This way," Janek said, pointing ahead. "It's a straight run for the perimeter fence. Up into the watchtower and down the other side."

He broke from the building, his rifle in his hands. Cade followed. Figures burst from the gloom, weapons up and firing. Cade was certain Janek took some hits, but if he did the cyborg ignored them and just kept going. His rifle swung in the direction of the armed men, spitting fire, the stream of slugs burning through flesh and bone and knocking the mercs to the ground.

As they neared the fence, Janek planted himself close to the base of the watchtower.

"Go!" he yelled at Cade, then turned his rifle on the figures converging on the area. He dragged grenades from his pouch and tossed them with unerring accuracy. The subsequent explosions dropped a number of men and drove the others into cover.

By this time Cade was over the fence and heading for the trees, and Janek lobbed a final grenade, then followed. Together they broke for the trees, hearing the angry buzz and whack of pursuing slugs.

After they hit the tree line, they pushed directly into the cover of the drooping branches and tangled thicket. Cade gagged as he breathed in the stench of decay.

"It might be bad," Janek pointed out, "but it's preferable to getting shot, I figure."

"Jesus," Cade gasped. "I might argue that point with you if I had the breath to spare."

"Just one of the drawbacks of being human," the cybo quipped. "You have to breathe."

"Yeah, yeah," Cade said. "Spare me the commercial for Cybo Tech."

Janek smirked in satisfaction.

He pushed his way through the dense mass of foliage, his directional functions keeping him on the same trail he'd followed on his way in.

Cade, keeping an eye on the trail behind them, kept in close contact with the cyborg. He trusted Janek's ability to get them clear of the base, but took account of the fact that on his way in the cyborg didn't have hostile forces at his back.

"You spotted any yet, T.J.?"

"Uh-uh, but they're out there. Those suckers won't quit. We've loused up their perfect plans, and they'll trail us to the back door of hell if they have to."

"They'll have to do it on foot," Janek said, "because I put their chopper out of commission."

Cade smiled. That would cause some bad-mouthing among Tane's crew. The merc leader would lose some credibility with Cade's escape. He'd be even more determined to stop Cade and Janek now.

Just then Janek stopped without warning, raising a hand. Cade pressed close to a thick tree trunk and peered back into the gloom, straining to pick up sounds of pursuit.

Janek indicated a distant point. Watching it carefully, Cade picked up the silent movement as someone eased through the foliage. He shouldered the rifle, squinting through the sight. He saw the armed figure swim into focus. Cade moved the barrel a fraction, leading the target. He waited until he had a comparatively clear shot, then gently eased back on the trigger. The rifle cracked sharply, and the muzzle lifted slightly as the bullet exited. Cade kept the sight on the target and was rewarded by the figure jerking back, slamming into a tree at his back and then pitching facedown on the forest floor.

"Pretty good, T.J.," Janek said softly. "Took your time, but you got there. Now let's set a pace and keep moving."

They moved on again, pushing deeper into the forested terrain, and the dense thicket closed in around them. Cade was still suffering the effects of the Chemlands stench. The pervading smell was inescapable. As they pushed deeper in, their pursuers fell farther behind. Light began to penetrate, exposing the decaying tangle of foliage, the twisted mutations that had once been normal, healthy trees. A thin mist rose from the spongy floor, curling around their feet as they passed. Cade spotted dark, lurking shapes underfoot and was thankful when they scurried out of his path. He had no desire to come face-to-face with any of the forest creatures.

They could hear the continuing sounds of pursuit. Lukas Tane and his mercs were still with them. The sounds rose and fell, sometimes seeming closer, then drifting away into the distance.

A crackle of autofire erupted without warning, and streams of slugs whipped through the foliage around Cade and Janek. Pale slivers of wood burst from a trunk close by Cade's head, stinging his cheek. He put on a spurt of speed that drew him level with Janek.

"What?" the cybo asked. "You see one with your name on it?"

Cade ignored the gibe. He pushed forward, following Janek's directions, plunging into a dense thicket. The thorny branches clawed at his clothes and flesh, and he envied Janek's immunity to pain.

He caught the cyborg's warning yell even as he picked up the soft whoosh of an incoming mortar shell. Cade dropped to a crouch, sheltering against a gnarled tree trunk. The mortar exploded with a sharp crack and lifted a chunk of forest floor. Clods of earth and torn vegetation rained down over the Justice cops, while swirling smoke drifted across the area.

Janek had picked up the mortar's delivery point. He ranged in with his rifle and let go with a sustained burst, placing his shots within a prescribed area. He heard one man yell in pain. Others thrashed around as they burrowed back into the thicket to avoid the incoming fire.

"You okay?" Janek asked.

Cade pushed to his feet, bracing himself against the trunk, the rifle to his shoulder as he spotted a tight group of mercs emerging from cover yards away from where the mortar had come.

His hard-driven shots dropped one man dead in his tracks and wounded another. The remaining mercs scattered, throwing a volley of loose shots as they dispersed.

"I am now," Cade growled.

"Let's move on," Janek suggested, and they broke cover to make for the deepest part of the thicket. Janek was in the lead, his tough frame carving a way through without pause. His keen eyes were able to pick out the most solid ground yards ahead, so he managed to keep them moving without too much wasted time.

Cade lost track of how long they pounded through the thicket. He concentrated on Janek's broad back as the cyborg ploughed his way forward, ignoring the hostile vegetation.

It was Cade himself who picked up the trio of mercs running parallel with them.

"Janek, your right!" he called.

The cyborg turned his upper body without breaking stride and opened fire, punching a spurting hole through the throat of one merc.

The others returned fire. They were carrying heavy-caliber machine rifles capable of delivering devastating, continuous volleys. They laid down a deadly stream of shots that began to shred the thicket round the Justice cops.

"Split," Janek yelled over his shoulder, ducking as bullets pounded the trees around him.

Cade swung left, diving into the foliage. Too late he spotted the gleam of water directly ahead, and before he could change direction he sank up to his knees in the slimy pool. He twisted his upper body around in time to see one of the pursuing mercs burst out of the thicket.

Cade's rifle arced up, and he peered through the sight at his target. The weapon fired, and the merc was knocked off his feet as the slug chewed a bloody hole in his shoulder. He still attempted to return fire, dragging his sagging machine rifle on line one-handed. But his effort was wasted as Cade triggered again, this time taking him out for good with a headshot.

Dragging himself out of the foul-smelling pool, Cade crossed to the far side of the clearing, then took a reckless dive into the foliage as he heard more of the mercs closing in behind him.

He ignored the clawing thorns and the sticky cling of unseen objects that crawled across his body. He figured it was wise not to wonder what they were.

The rattle of shots accelerated his progress, and he heard the hail of slugs burning the air above his head, clipping the foliage and timber.

On his stomach, he crawled into the depths of the thicket. The floor of the forest felt soft and spongy beneath him. Cade could have sworn the damn thing was alive. One thing he could agree on. The Chemlands were hellish—like nothing else he'd ever experienced.

There was a sudden, tumultuous exchange of fire. The racket seemed to come from all sides. Cade sat upright, his rifle at the ready. Just as suddenly the firing ceased and the forest around him fell silent.

Janek reappeared, striding through the thicket like some creature from a horror movie. His clothing was filthy and tattered, his face streaked where the makeup had rubbed off. Apart from that he looked fine. No agitation. No sweat. The cyborg was his normal, in-control self.

"I think we've lost them for the time being," he said, staring down at Cade. "What are you doing down there, T.J.? You lost something?"

"Only my sanity," Cade replied, sleeving dirt from his face as he climbed to his feet. "And don't give up on those mercs so easy."

Janek turned, plodding on through the thicket, his powerful hands ripping aside tangles of gnarled and knotted branches.

"Chopper's close now. We should be there shortly."

They covered another quarter mile before the thicket thinned out and the terrain began to rise in a series of uneven steps.

Pushing hard, Cade kept up with the relentlessly tireless cyborg. His whole body ached, muscles screaming in protest against the pressure he was putting on them. The sweat pouring down his face burned through the cuts and bruises. He figured that in a few more hours he was going to be stiffer than a burned-out service droid.

Janek reached into his top pocket and pulled out the signaling device. He pressed the button that would give Kate the signal to start the chopper's engine.

At the base of the slope armed figures moved into view. Tane's mercs had picked up the trail again.

The first indication of their persistence was sporadic gunfire. A stream of slugs peppered the slope, kicking up dirt and chipping rocks.

Janek took out the last of his grenades. He pulled the pins and threw the grenades downslope. The detonations failed to injure anyone, but the effect was still positive, as Tane's men scattered, their offensive fire faltering then dying as they ducked for cover.

Digging in his heels, Cade made it to the top of the slope. He trailed close behind Janek.

The thump of the chopper's rotors reached Cade's ears before he saw the craft. He was too weary to figure out how Janek had managed to arrange for the engine to be up and running.

The hatch door swung open. Janek grabbed Cade's arm and shoved him into the chopper. Cade sprawled across the floor. He sensed Janek stepping over him and dropping into the pilot's seat. Janek locked the hatch, then pushed the power to max, working the stick and foot controls. The chopper lifted off immediately.

Cade sat up, shaking the mist from his eyes. He leaned his back against the bulkhead and only then realized there was someone in the copilot's seat.

Slim figure.

Red hair.

"Hey!" he said, reaching out to spin the seat around.

"Hello, T.J.," Kate Bannion said, giving him her best smile.

Cade stared at her for a moment. Out of the corner of his eye he noticed Janek hunching down in his seat, trying to make his tall frame disappear.

"So I'm not around, and there's a conspiracy behind my back," Cade growled. "Janek, you just have to learn to resist beautiful women."

8

Using the helicopter's on-board vid-phone, Cade called up Milt Schuberg of the NYPD. Schuberg was an old friend, one Cade knew and trusted.

"What the hell happened to your face?" Schuberg asked when he came on. "Got to admit, T.J., it's an improvement." Then he got serious. "What's going on? There's all kinds of shit flying around. Seems you've been stepping on some pretty high-powered toes. Right now you ain't exactly flavor-of-the-month."

"I'll keep that in mind," Cade said. "Listen, Milt, there anything I should watch out for?"

"Don't go near your place or Kate's. No kidding, T.J., you are hot. Can't find out where the orders are coming from, but it's way over our heads."

"Thanks for the tip, Milt. Watch out, yourself. There's something big brewing, and the players aren't fussy who gets hurt."

"Will do, big feller. Hey, T.J., stay in touch."

Cade cut the connection and looked over at Janek.

"We have to land somewhere, sometime," Janek said matter-of-factly. "Any ideas?"

"How are we for firepower?"

"I picked up enough to see us through the week," Janek replied. "Why?"

"How about *we* do a little pushing for a change," Cade said. "Like dropping in at Amosin?"

"Haven't you had enough?" Kate asked. "Out of one mess, and you want to jump right into another?"

"I'm not doing this for the fun of it," Cade said. "Right now I'm thinking about George Takagi. All he was doing was his job...and it got him killed."

Kate touched his arm, her face gentle. "And I'm just trying to keep you alive."

"Cut it out, you two," Janek said. "You'll have me in tears."

The cyborg leaned forward to tap in coordinates that displayed a map of the New York environs. He fed in more information, and the image altered, focusing on a magnified area of the map.

"That's it," Janek said. "Amosin's complex. That's where they have their robotics division. There's also a weapons section. Amos Sinclair, the guy running the corporation, has his estate inside the complex. I read about it once. The place is out of this world. He's got everything he'll ever need there."

"Isn't he reputed to be a recluse?" Kate asked. "Hardly ever leaves the place. When he does, he goes by his own transport direct to his destination and then straight back."

"Sounds a likable kind of guy," Cade murmured. He was opening the bag of weapons Janek had left in the helicopter. "Wasn't he involved in some political fuss a few years back?"

"That's right," Kate said. "We ran an article on it. He's got some pretty radical views on the way the country's being run. Doesn't like the administration or the way it's letting the U.S. down worldwide. Sinclair was going on about it being time for a hard-line government, one that would push the U.S. back to the top of the league. He was trying to get some candidate into the running for future president. Some hard-liner spitting fire and damnation."

"Problem was the guy had the charisma of a week-old sweaty sock," Cade said. "He might have been a hardass, but he didn't even get the backing of the skid-row winos."

"Sinclair backed out of the political scene after that," Kate said. "Haven't heard much about him since. Hey, you guys, is he involved in this business?"

Cade hefted a powerful SMG he'd pulled from the bag.

"That's what we're going to find out," he said.

THEY LANDED the helicopter at a small airfield about twenty miles from the Amosin complex. There was a local car-rental agency at the field. Using Kate's credit card, they hired a nondescript 4x4 and loaded all their gear into the truck. Before they left, Janek shut down the chopper's power plant and even disconnected the radio and vid-phone so there were no signals being transmitted. If someone wanted to track them, they would do it eventually. He was attempting to put off the hour for as long as possible.

"What about my credit card?" Kate asked when they were already rolling north along the highway that would lead them to Amosin.

"Let's hope they haven't covered that," Cade said, not too convincingly.

The plan was to drop Kate off at a small motel so she could check in with Milt Schuberg, while Cade and Janek went for the Amosin complex.

They didn't even have the opportunity to locate a motel. Half an hour after they left the airfield, they picked up a tail. Janek spotted it in the rearview mirror.

"They must have half the state on their payroll,"
Cade grumbled. "Come on, Janek, let's get out of
here."

Janek trod on the gas pedal. The 4x4 picked up with
surprising speed, and he held it on a steady course as it
hurtled along the highway.

"Hang on," he said. "I can make a left about three
hundred yards along. Gets us on a back road we can use
to get us to Amosin."

"They'll have that covered, Janek," Cade yelled
above the roar of the truck's motor. "Don't delude
yourself. This bunch knows how to play the game."

"Okay, okay," Janek snapped. "You're so damn
smart, you do the navigating."

"Take that cutoff," Cade said. "But leave it to the
last second so our tail overshoots. Then come out fast
and get me on *his* tail."

Janek made a sound like a harsh chuckle. "Sneaky,
Thomas," he said. "I love it."

He tromped down harder on the pedal, and the truck
surged forward. Using his perfect timing and coordination, the cyborg calculated his turn precisely. He
barely slowed before whipping the 4x4 off the highway
and around onto the side road. Tires howled in protest
as Janek guided the truck into the curve. The tail car
shot by, and its brakes locked as the driver realized his
error. The car lurched back and forth across the highway, swaying dangerously. It covered a couple of hundred yards before the wheelman had it under control.

By then he was too late.

Janek knocked the truck into reverse and rolled out
of the side road, then took the 4x4 forward. Cade had
already lowered his window, leaning out with the SMG
cocked and ready.

As the truck bore down on them, the occupants of the tail car abandoned the vehicle. Doors sprang open and armed men spilled out across the highway. They started firing wildly, too concerned with their own safety to even aim properly.

Cade opened up with his SMG, raking the rear of the tail car with a volley. The magazine he'd loaded contained a combination of steel-jackets and tracers. The slugs ripped through the car's steel bodywork, tearing open the fuel tank, and the tracers did the rest. Just as Janek rolled the truck past the car, it blew in a ball of orange flame and black smoke. The fireball swallowed the car and spread across the highway, scorching the side of the 4x4 as it shot by. The roof of the truck was peppered with flying debris. The gush of fire and smoke rose into the bright, cloudless sky.

Janek pushed the truck to the limit. They were all aware that there would be more opposition. Amosin knew they were on their way. The vast organization had the means to throw up a great deal of interference.

It could—and it did.

More cars appeared behind them, swinging in behind the truck. This time they didn't hang back. With motors howling, they closed rapidly on the lone 4x4.

Autofire crackled. The truck's rear window blew in, showering them with glass.

Cade fired through the gap and blew a line of ragged holes across the hood of the lead vehicle. The driver eased back, allowing the second car to hold the close position. This one poured on the power and rammed the rear of the 4x4. The truck shuddered and slid until Janek brought it back under control. The pursuing driver repeated his maneuver, deliberately ramming the 4x4.

"That guy's either suicidal or one of those damn combat droids," Cade yelled.

"I don't care what he is," Janek snapped back. "Just stop him!"

Cade scrambled over the rear seat and crouched in the truck's rear compartment. He wedged himself against the rear corner, watching the advancing tail car. As it loomed closer for a third strike, Cade leaned forward and triggered the SMG's magazine at the windshield, raking it the width of the vehicle. The windshield exploded in the faces of the occupants. The man beside the driver flung up both hands as his face became shredded and bloody. The driver didn't flinch, despite the fact that his chest and face were lacerated by the flying glass. Cade caught a glimpse of dully polished titanium steel beneath the shredded artificial flesh.

"Kate, in the bag. Grenades. The round ones," Cade yelled.

She passed him a few. Cade pulled the pin on one and tossed it. The grenade hit the car's hood and bounced off. It struck the highway and exploded, and the second tail car swerved. The cyborg driving the lead car eased off when he realized Cade's intention, but the cop had already primed another grenade. This one went in through the car's shattered windshield and detonated inside the vehicle. The lead car blew wide open, scattering debris across the highway. The combat droid lost control as the blast buffeted it. Before it could regain that control, the car lurched to the right, hit the grass shoulder and flipped. A man's bloodied body was thrown out of the rear, and it smashed facedown on the highway. Before the driver in the other tail car could react, he drove over the body.

"T.J.!" Janek yelled.

Glancing over his shoulder, Cade peered through the truck's windshield. A roadblock was being set up ahead of them.

"You want me to ram them?" Janek asked.

Cade glanced at Kate. She was staring through the windshield at the line of vehicles ahead and the armed figures waiting behind them. It didn't show on her face, but he could guess what she was thinking, and he couldn't lay her life on the line with such a reckless move.

"Ease off, Janek," he said. "We'll let them think they've got us cold. Let them get us in to see the top honchos in this deal, then we can make our move."

Janek slowed the truck and rolled to a stop at the roadblock.

Cade felt Kate's eyes on him.

"Sometimes, T. J. Cade, you talk the worst load of crap I ever heard," she said.

"Please," Janek said stiffly. "I wasn't programmed to listen to such language. And I only enjoy it when female cyborgs talk dirty to me."

THIRTY MINUTES LATER, Cade, Janek and Kate, under armed escort, were taken from the car that had brought them into the Amosin complex and walked across a wide courtyard decorated with beds of lush flowers and ornate fountains. At one side of the courtyard was a wide, curving lawn, complete with shrubs and trees. Birds sang in the branches, and there appeared to be an abundance of wildlife moving in and out of the shrubbery. There was a look of perfection to the setup that made Cade look twice. He realized that the wildlife scene was a highly sophisticated holographic image.

The courtyard gave way to a spacious patio with a huge swimming pool. At a stone barbecue a gleaming service droid cooked sizzling steaks.

"Is that real steak?" Kate whispered as they were ushered past.

"Just be our luck if it's another holograph," Cade said.

"It's real, Marshal Cade. Go ahead, take one. See for yourself."

Cade located the owner of the voice.

The man stood just outside the curving expanse of a picture window that opened onto the patio. Inside the wide, low-ceilinged room pale carpet covered the floor. The furnishings were expensive and looked extremely comfortable. Even from where he was standing, Cade could see real leather armchairs and loungers.

Cade recognized the speaker as Amos Sinclair. He remembered seeing the man on TV news programs. Sinclair had to be at least fifty. He was in good condition, slim, fit and tanned, his dark hair just showing signs of graying. The man's face, lean and taut, had a predatory look. His pale blue-gray eyes were fixed on Cade. They told a great deal about the man. He was hard. Uncompromising. He might have been a recluse, although he certainly didn't look like one.

Sinclair stepped forward, checking out Janek and Kate as he approached.

"It appears our late, unlamented friend Culver made a foolish mistaken when he took you on, Cade. The man obviously didn't realize how strongly you would retaliate. It's done now, so there's no point in worrying about it. At least we have you contained now." Sinclair smiled. "You had us worried for a while. Your mistake was deciding to come here. Did you really believe you could have achieved anything?"

"I've got you out in the open," Cade said. "All I need now are the others...."

Sinclair smiled. "What others?"

"Try Colonel Clayton Munro and Colonel Edwin Poole," Janek said. "That jog your memory?"

Cade noticed movement in the room behind Sinclair, and a low murmur of voices reached his ear.

"Let's put faces to the names," Cade said. "Or don't you have the nerve to show yourselves?"

Amos Sinclair chuckled. "I think he's challenging you boys. Let the man have his moment."

Cade watched the men step out of the room into the sunlight. They were in civilian clothing, but there was no hiding the military bearing.

"You have to admit the man's good," Sinclair said. "You could do with someone like him in your outfit, Clay."

Clayton Munro, tall and dark haired, glared at Sinclair.

"Him? A goddamn cop?"

"A Justice marshal, Clay. More than a street cop."

"Are you the T. J. Cade who was in the Marine Corps?" asked Edwin Poole. He took Cade's angry look for a yes. "This is no dogface, Clay. He was in the strike against the Islamic Federation nuclear facility during the war. Did some time on the asteroids, as well."

"For Christ's sake," Munro exploded. "This fucker has spent the last couple of days causing us all kinds of problems, and you want to give him a testimonial? Amos is offering him steak. What next? Why don't you ask him if he wants to be President?"

"That's not up for grabs," Sinclair said softly. The gleam in his eyes told Munro he was not amused by the man's final remark.

"Ah!" Munro muttered, and went back inside the house.

"What *are* we going to do with them?" Poole asked, looking at Sinclair.

"Get rid of them, of course," Sinclair snapped. "I thought that was plain enough. That is, after we have extracted all the information they possess. From Cade's remarks, it's plain they've picked up a disturbing amount of knowledge about our affairs. We still go ahead. It's too late to stop things, anyway. I don't intend waiting another month. All we need from these three is whether they've passed any of their information to others. If they have, we could find ourselves with difficult situations on our hands at the wrong time. Once we have control, it won't matter. But until we do, I can't have any of our key people put at risk."

"By key people you mean the cops on your payroll?" Cade said. "And who else?"

"Apart from your cut-price colonels," Kate said, unable to contain her anger, "just what is it this time, Sinclair? You tried to push some puppet candidate for the White House once before and failed. Is this another of your games?"

"Games!" Sinclair thundered, his calm exterior exploding into righteous anger. "Do you think this is just a casual affair, young woman? Don't you realize what's at stake here? The enormity of what we're doing?"

"Why don't you tell us?" Cade said evenly, attracting Sinclair's attention. "Make us understand, Sinclair."

"Look around you," Sinclair said. "You'll understand soon enough. Look and see how this nation is falling apart, crumbling by the day. Crime in the streets. A faltering economy. A nation in decay. America's standing in the world at an all-time low. Our influence waning. There was a time when the United States stood for strength and democracy. The world jumped when this country spoke. We had power. We guided the weak and held back the oppressors. Not anymore—and that has to change. We have to redress the balance of power in our favor."

"And you're the man to do it?" Cade said.

"Sneer all you want, Cade. But yes, I am. This country needs a strong leader. Not a weakling like Grainger."

"You're forgetting one thing. President Grainger was the people's choice. They voted him in. You won't give the country that option?"

"There are times when the needs of the many have to be decided without the ballot box."

Cade shook his head in disbelief. "Now we get to it. You want to put the country back on track by installing an administration based on dictatorship. That it? Overturn the government and put yourself in power. To hell with the people, Amos Sinclair for President."

"You'll never do it," Kate said. "The power structure is too strong to allow a coup to be successful."

"No, Kate, I think they could do it," Janek said. He was facing Sinclair as he spoke. "If their plan works, they could pull it off."

"What plan?" Cade asked.

"Skylance. If they get control of the Skylance weapons satellite, they can hold the country to ransom—and threaten the rest of the world."

Sinclair smiled. "Congratulations," he said to Janek. "Your cyborg partner is very astute, Cade. I may decide to keep him alive. Let my own specialist check him over. I've always admired Cybo Tech's success. Amosin Robotics have never quite kept pace with the sophisticated advances Cybo Tech seems to have made."

"I'd say you've cornered the market in combat droids with antisocial tendencies," Cade commented.

"Very good, Marshal Cade. I do like a man with a sense of humor. Especially when he's in a tricky situation."

Edwin Poole cleared his throat.

"All this sounds fine," he said, "but I think we should get back to the matter at hand. We're losing time, Amos. The advance team has to be in position by this evening, and we need to move our inside people into the right places before morning."

"Yes, you're right," Sinclair said. His manner changed abruptly. "What about Tane and his people?"

"The reserve chopper is already on the way back with them. The base doesn't figure in our plans any longer. We would have abandoned it, anyway. Cade and his friends just forced our hand a little."

Sinclair nodded. He glared at Cade. "You cost us some valuable men."

"The way they went down, Sinclair, you're better off without them."

"I doubt Tane will view it that way. He's a man with an extremely nasty temperament. Maybe I'd be doing you a favor if I had you killed here and now. At least it would be quick."

Amos Sinclair picked up a telephone and punched in a number. He spoke quickly to whoever answered, then replaced the receiver.

"Edwin, you and Clayton carry on. I'll remain here and coordinate as planned. Cade and his friends will be dealt with in due time."

"What about Tane?" Poole asked.

"Don't you worry about our mercenary friend," Sinclair said. "He's in this for the money. As long as I keep feeding him, he'll do what I say."

Poole gestured to one of the armed men. "Get over to the helicopter pad. Tell the crew I want a chopper ready for immediate takeoff. Landon to pilot. He knows exactly where we're going."

Poole faced Cade. "I'm genuinely sorry you can't be persuaded to join us, Cade. A man with your military record would go far. No second thoughts?"

"Second thoughts? Sure. But you wouldn't like to hear them, Colonel."

Poole's face paled for a moment, and his lips set in a tight line. He pulled himself upright, his shoulders squared. His eyes searched Cade's face and he nodded to himself slowly. Then he turned and strode away, inside the house and out of sight.

Sinclair snapped his fingers at the service droid, still faithfully preparing the steaks at the barbecue.

"You can leave those now and fetch me a drink."

The droid nodded and hurried away.

"Is that how you expect the country to respond?" Kate asked. "Amos Sinclair clicks his fingers, and we all jump? I don't think so."

"Consider the alternative, my dear," Sinclair said. "There won't be any choice."

"This guy's crazy, T.J.," Kate said. "He really believes he's going to do it. Force the government to hand power over to him and his colonels."

"Surprising what the hot weather brings out of the woodwork," Janek said.

A moment later, realizing the deliberate insult, the armed man behind Janek rammed the muzzle of his weapon into the cyborg's side, and Janek turned to glare at him.

The service droid reappeared, carrying a silver tray with a tall glass balanced on it. The droid was followed by a man dressed in a white suit, and he in turn was flanked by a pair of combat droids wearing black jumpsuits. Both droids wore shoulder rigs holding autopistols.

The newcomer joined Sinclair. His angular face, topped by dark hair slicked back across his head, was marked by a pattern of puckered scars down the left side.

"He's all yours," Sinclair said, indicating Janek. "One of Cybo Tech's finest. He's called Janek."

The scarred man circled Janek, studying him closely.

"I'm not too impressed by his choice in clothing," he commented, flicking a finger at Janek's filthy, tattered combat suit.

"Who is this joker?" Janek asked, indignation heavy in his voice. He didn't like being inspected like a downgraded service droid.

"Jubal Casull," Sinclair said. "Head of Amosin's robotics division. I believe you've had contact with some of his creations."

"If you mean those half-assed combat droids, I'm not impressed," Janek said.

"Does it always react like this?" Casull asked.

"If you want answers, ask Janek," Cade said. "He doesn't need my permission to speak."

"A liberated machine," Casull said. "That's something new."

Janek glanced across at Cade, raising his eyes in exasperation.

"Jubal, get Janek into the secure lab. Keep him there until we have the operation under way, then get back here. I need you to assist me. Take the girl with you. That will ensure Janek behaves. He won't put her life at risk."

"Cee Sixer, Cee Ten," Casull said, "escort these two to the lab complex."

The combat droids responded immediately. Easing the autopistols from their holsters, they covered Kate, pushing her ahead of them.

"They may be half-assed," Casull said to Janek, "but don't be fooled into believing they won't kill her if I give the word."

Janek understood only too well. He fell in beside Kate as Jubal Casull led them across the patio, leaving Cade alone with Sinclair and his armed gunmen.

Overhead a civilian helicopter rose above the estate and set course for New York.

"You'll find my lab interesting," Casull said conversationally as he led the way through the Amosin complex. "I have some of the finest equipment in existence. Our combat droids are considered the most efficient the military has ever purchased."

"You create them to kill," Kate said, "and not just enemy soldiers. They even came to my apartment and tried to kill me."

"Exceptional circumstances call for drastic measures," Casull said without a trace of regret.

Janek had been studying the man as they walked and now spoke up. "How long have you had the bionic arms?" he asked.

"I wondered how long it would take for you to notice. Almost four years now. My natural limbs were severed in an accident. So I made use of my own expertise and created my own replacement arms."

He held up his arms, flexing his fingers.

"With the skills you have, why waste it all on a damn-fool scheme like Sinclair's?" Janek asked.

"Because I believe the man is right. The country needs a new kind of government, one willing to drag us out of the mess we're in."

"Or push us into a deeper one," Kate said.

Casull cast her an annoyed look but didn't bother answering. They continued on through the sprawling complex until they reached a three-story building constructed from dark glass and steel. The entrance was a gleaming airlock. Casull punched in an access code, then stepped back as the airlock went into its opening sequence.

"The facility has to be kept sterile," Casull explained. "Cybernetics requires pure atmospheres during implantation of highly sensitive electronic function modes. Everything must be kept clean. So the interior is kept isolated from the outside world."

The airlock swung open, and they stepped inside. The door closed and they were left inside the lock itself. Gleaming steel and ceramic surrounded them. The soft click of electronics filled the air. A soft hiss preceded an enveloping mist that jetted over them, followed by the bathing glow of ultraviolet light. Fresh air was pumped into the lock, and automatic checks finally lit up a display panel that gave them the all clear.

The inner airlock door slid open. Ahead of them stretched a long corridor. The left wall was composed of clear, toughened Plexiglas, through which could be seen the Amosin complex they had just come through. The opposite wall held recessed cabinets in which were holographic images of different Amosin Robotic creations. There was also a bank of elevator doors. Partway along Janek saw a flight of stairs leading to the upper floors.

"Later I may take you on a tour of the facility."

"I can't wait," Kate muttered dryly.

"But first," Casull said with undisguised pride in his voice, "I want you to see where it all takes place. My laboratory. The birthplace of my robots."

9

Cade had seen the first chopper take off from somewhere in the complex. Thirty minutes later he watched a larger machine fly in and land, and something told him Lukas Tane and his mercenaries had returned to Amosin from the hidden base out near Placid Lake.

The arrival of the helicopter made him realize it was time to make his move. Amos Sinclair claimed he could control Tane, but Cade didn't share his confidence. Tane had already been made to look a damn fool because of Cade and Janek. The merc was going to be in a vengeful frame of mind, liable to shoot Cade on sight and argue the point later.

Cade slowly and unobtrusively inspected the area from where he was sitting in one of the pool loungers.

Sinclair was busy on the telephone. He'd been continuously occupied since Jubal Casull had returned from wherever he'd taken Janek and Kate. While Sinclair spoke on the phone, Casull used a dictopad to make notes. There were three armed guards keeping watch over Cade, though they had relaxed due to the length of time they'd all been waiting.

Without making any sudden moves, Cade stood up. He immediately attracted the attention of the guards.

"Hey, you want to stay put," one suggested.

"The man offered me a steak," Cade said. "Might be my last, so the hell with you."

The guard crossed over to confront the Justice cop.

"So? You going to shoot me?" Cade asked. "Sinclair needs to talk to me."

"Let him go," Casull said irritably. "What harm can he do? Just watch him."

The guard trailed behind Cade as he approached the barbecue. The service droid, glad that it was at last going to have a customer, snapped upright.

"How can I help you, sir?"

"Steak, medium rare, straight off the grill," Cade said.

"Anything with it, sir?"

"No. Just as it comes."

From somewhere beyond the house, alarm sirens went off.

Jubal Casull raised his head, anxiety in his eyes.

"My complex," he said. "Something may have gone wrong."

"You better check," Sinclair snapped, breaking off his conversation. "Decker, go with him," he said to one of the guards.

One down, Cade thought.

Casull dropped the dictopad on the small table beside Sinclair and hurried off, followed by the guard.

Sinclair returned to his telephone conversation.

The service droid hummed to itself as it cooked Cade's steak. It sizzled hotly on the grill as the steaming juices oozed from the meat and dropped onto the red-hot syntho-coal beneath.

"That looks about right," Cade said.

"Perhaps a little more, sir," the droid suggested.

"It'll be fine," Cade said firmly.

The droid picked up a plastic plate and deftly deposited Cade's steak on it. It handed the plate over.

"Now that's what I call a steak," Cade said, letting the guard catch a whiff of the rich meat.

The guard felt his taste buds start to salivate. He watched the steak as Cade held it up for him to see.

Cade pushed the still-sizzling slab of meat into the guard's face, clapping a hand behind his head to hold it against the steak. The guard's yell of pain was muffled by the meat squashed against his lips, burning them. He let go of the SMG he was carrying as he tried to drag the steak away from his flesh. Cade dropped the plate and grabbed the SMG. He saw the other guard coming around, attracted by the noise. Cade swung up the SMG and triggered it fast, sending an arc of hot lead that chipped the patio first, then climbed to stitch a bloody row of holes in the guard's stomach and chest. The guard staggered back, then lost his balance and crashed down on the tiles surrounding the pool.

Behind Cade the service droid began making excited sounds, throwing its gleaming arms in the air.

Out of the corner of his eye Cade saw the burned guard lunging at him, despite his injured face. Cade ducked below the man's outstretched arms, then thrust upright again. The guard was tossed over Cade's back and crashed down on the smoking grill of the barbecue. His scream of agony completely unnerved the service droid, and it scuttled off across the patio in a panic.

The clatter of a chair attracted Cade's attention. He saw Sinclair running for the house. Cade went after him, but the industrialist slipped in through the sliding glass doors. Before Cade could reach the opening, the glass wall slid into place, blocking off the room.

Cade didn't bother trying to break through. By the time he did, Sinclair would be long gone.

He turned and ran across the patio toward the distant exit. He needed to get away from the area before Lukas Tane showed his face. As he passed the spot where Sinclair had been sitting during his telephone conversations, Cade noticed the dictopad Jubal Casull had been using. It was still on the small table. Hardly breaking his stride, Cade picked up the pad and slipped it into one of his pockets.

He skirted the pool and emerged in the wide courtyard with its holographic garden. He didn't head in the direction he'd been led when they arrived, but angled across toward the main complex area. Somewhere in there were Janek and Kate.

He was brought up short by the arrival of Tane and his mercs. They had burst into view from the patio area, seeking him, and opened fire the moment they set eyes on his distant figure. The scattering of shots, off target but close enough to alert him, decided Cade's immediate course of action. He cut off across the courtyard and ducked through an ornate archway.

He found himself on a curving drive leading in the direction of the main Amosin complex. Cade crossed the drive and used the cover of a low wall to hide his progress. The maneuver worked until the wall faded out, and he was left with an open area to cover before he would be able to use the first of the complex buildings. Throwing a quick glance over his shoulder, Cade saw that Tane and four of his mercs were already in sight, fanning out as they searched for him.

He broke away from the wall and made a dash for the building.

Halfway there he heard a yell, followed by the crackle of gunfire. The concrete around him was pockmarked by bullets, and Cade felt chips pepper his legs as he took off at a dead run, weaving erratically. Something plucked at his left sleeve, burning across the flesh of his arm. The pain spurred him on. Cade reached the cover of the building and kept on moving. He ran hard, ducking and turning in and out of the series of alleyways he found between the cluster of buildings.

His chest heaving, lungs burning, Cade flopped down in the shadow of a tank secured to the side of one building. His rest was shortlived. The pounding of combat boots on the concrete warned him of someone's approach.

Even as Cade was moving from cover, one of Tane's men skidded around the end of the building, laying his eyes on the cop almost immediately. The merc's hand went to the walkie-talkie clipped to his belt while his SMG swung into position.

Cade didn't hesitate. His own weapon crackled briefly, but with effective results. The short blast planted a stream of slugs in the merc's chest, flattening him against the wall before slamming him to the ground.

Cade moved on, pushing deeper into the complex.

The way ahead opened out as the cluster of buildings gave way to a broad drive leading to a glass-and-steel building standing on its own.

There was a blazing vehicle near the building, and Cade knew that somewhere along the line Janek was involved.

10

Jubal Casull keyed in the access code. The steel doors slid open to reveal the interior of his laboratory. The robotics expert gestured lightly, and Cee Ten prodded Kate with the autopistol, moving her into the lab. Janek followed, scanning the vast room with interest.

It was equipped with computer banks and an impressive array of electronic support consoles. On the right were glass-enclosed rooms where delicate microbionic operations could be carried out in isolation. A row of tubular booths lined one wall. Janek recognized them as syntho-flesh transmitters.

"You find it interesting, Janek?" Casull asked, watching his reactions closely.

"Yes," Janek replied. "It's just a pity that it's being wasted."

"Disapproval," Casull said. "I hope you're not going to bore me with too much righteous indignation. Instead, Janek, accept that we all have the right to choose our path. That's democracy after all."

"Democracy doesn't mean forcing your view on others."

"If we had the time, we could discuss this for hours," Casull said. "But this isn't the time for a lengthy discussion on semantics."

"Why don't we just kill them now?" Cee Ten asked.

"Save your aggression for the battlefield," Casull suggested. "Sometimes, Cee, you're a pain in the butt."

"Don't blame me," the droid said. "You keyed in my program. I'm only responding to that."

"What are you going to do with us?" Kate asked.

"Janek is too valuable to destroy," Casull said. "His development has gone beyond anything I've ever seen. I need time to study it, but right now I have other things to do. So you'll stay here until I'm free. On his own Janek would pose a threat, and I'm fully aware of his potential for violence. I need something that will restrain him. As long as you're here, under threat, Janek isn't going to cause much of a problem. He won't put you at risk. Right, Janek?"

Janek's lopsided shrug only produced a smile from Casull.

"That much I do understand about you, Janek. The woman means a lot to you and to Cade. You cannot—will not—place her knowingly in danger. That's why Cee Ten and Cee Sixer are going to keep you here. If you do try anything, they're under orders to kill Bannion. And believe me, they'll do it. Their standards of morality when it comes to killing innocents are far below yours."

"You'd better believe it," Cee Ten said tautly.

Janek glanced at the combat droid, holding his gaze.

Kate, who was watching, caught the cold gleam in Janek's eyes. It was an expression she'd never seen before. Janek had always shown her friendliness and genuine affection. The coldness in his eyes and the totally alien expression on his face scared her. She felt a shiver of apprehension run down her spine. This was a side to Janek he had kept concealed before, and it was something Kate didn't want to see.

"I have to leave you now, but I'll be back in a while. Once we have the operation under way. Then we can get down to business. I look forward to it."

Casull strode from the lab, and the steel doors slid shut behind him.

Janek turned and caught Kate's eye.

"You might as well find somewhere to sit down, Kate," he suggested.

Kate shrugged, then wandered across the lab and slumped in a padded seat. The lab, with its bright lights and clinical atmosphere, was distinctly inhuman. It was a place for machines and unfeeling personalities. There was nothing to do with the real world here. No flesh and blood. No understanding. No...

She suddenly felt embarrassed by her thoughts. Because she was classing Janek along with the other droids and their surroundings. He was different. She knew it, and felt guilty for allowing herself to lapse from that knowledge.

Maybe it was because she was scared. Not knowing what was going to happen.

To her. To Janek. To Cade.

Kate's thoughts drifted. She felt weary. The physical exertions and emotional strain of the past hours were catching up with her suddenly. Despite the situation she was in, she didn't feel like fighting the tiredness, even though she could feel her eyes getting heavy. Her head sagged ... the long minutes blurred ... time lost meaning. ...

"You want to stand still!"

Kate jerked out of her half sleep. She looked across to where Cee Sixer had confronted Janek. The combat droid was threatening Janek with its weapon.

"They must allow you to watch a lot of TV," Janek remarked lightly. "Put the gun away, Sixer, you look stupid."

"You'll see how stupid I look when I blow you away."

"Casull wouldn't be too happy if you did that. Look, all I was doing was taking a look around. You've got the damn guns, and I can't do much while you have Kate in here. So keep your hair on." Janek examined Cee Sixer's dark crop. "Not that you've got much to lose. Is it supposed to be like that, or are you the first droid to go bald?"

Sixer scowled at him. He turned to stare at Cee Ten.

"Forget it," Ten snapped. "Can't you see, he's only trying to annoy you."

"Well he is," Sixer grumbled. "These Cybo Tech droids are all the same. Too much brain."

"Nobody could ever accuse you of that, Sixer," Janek said softly, his tone needling and accompanied by a trace of a smirk.

Cee Sixer gave a snarl of anger, swinging back to face Janek. The combat droid's overreaction was exactly what Janek had been expecting.

His right arm shot out, grabbing hold of Sixer's gunhand. He pulled and twisted at the same time, spinning Sixer around, drawing the droid up close. His powerful fingers bit into Sixer's hand, crushing through the flexi-coat of steel under the skin, searching for the control sensors. Sixer's grip on the autopistol slackened as Janek's probing fingertips dug in deep. The weapon slipped free. Janek caught it, finger stroking the trigger as he tracked the weapon in on Cee Ten, watching the droid's own weapon coming on line. Janek got to it first, his responses microseconds ahead of the slower combat droid. The autopistol exploded with sound as Janek fired three times in quick succession. The steel-jacketed bullets blasted in through Ten's left eye, tunneling deep into his electronic brain and terminating him in an instant. Cee Ten stumbled back, all coordination gone. He arched across one of the computer banks, a flailing fist crashing through a monitor. The gun in his hand began firing, sending a volley of slugs across the lab.

"Down!" Janek yelled at Kate.

She had already realized the danger she was in and rolled off the seat to stretch prone across the floor. Once she had found some cover, she looked around frantically for something to use as a weapon or a diversion. Then she slowly began to inch forward.

Janek had his hands full as Cee Sixer fought back. The combat droid reached up with its left hand and caught hold of Janek's suit. It yanked hard, bending forward, and threw Janek over its shoulder. The cyborg hit the floor, rolling swiftly to avoid Sixer's slashing foot. It caught him on the left shoulder, and the impact flipped Janek on his back, jarring the autopistol from his hand.

Janek twisted frantically, making a grab for the weapon, but Sixer was on him too quickly. The combat droid smashed down across Janek's back, wrapping both arms around Janek's throat and levering him up. Janek felt the pressure building along his lower back. He planted both hands on the floor, increasing the pressure in his system so he was able to resist Sixer's attack. For a moment they were locked in a stalemate, each utilizing its strength to the limit.

Balancing on his left hand, Janek caught hold of Sixer's right wrist and pulled the droid's arm free. He continued the movement, concentrating all his power in his right arm. Suddenly he yanked hard on Sixer's right arm.

The combat droid's response was to lock its upper body, resisting, which was just what Janek had expected. He continued his forward movement, and the extreme pressure dragged Sixer's arm from its shoulder socket. Syntho-flesh shredded and function modes tore apart as Sixer's arm was ripped from its body.

The combat droid, reacting to its coded instructions, released Janek, pushed to its feet and went looking for a weapon to compensate for the loss of its arm. Sixer's eyes located the discarded autopistol. The droid went for the gun. Even as it bent to scoop it up off the floor, Kate rushed in to snatch it up as Janek lunged at the droid from behind.

Locked together, they crashed headfirst into a cabinet and became enveloped in a cascade of crackling sparks as power lines were severed. Janek recovered first, hauling himself upright as Sixer stumbled awkwardly to its feet. The droid's facial syntho-flesh was torn and melted from the heat of the electrical discharge, and gleaming steel showed beneath the charred covering. Janek hit out at Sixer, his solid fist catching the droid beneath the jaw. Sixer fell back into the depths of the shattered cabinet. The eruption of electrical energy, attracted to its steel body, bathed Sixer in a brilliant glow. The heat ignited its clothing and shriveled its flesh. Somewhere inside Sixer's body shell there was a sharp crackle. It began to kick and squirm, its legs and single arm windmilling out of synch, head rolling from side to side.

Janek turned away. Kate was holding the autopistol in a rigid two-handed grip, looking as though she would never let it go. He walked over to her and extended his hand. When she put the weapon in it, he checked it for a full clip.

"Don't go risking your life for me, Kate," he said sternly, but his eyes were gentle on her face.

"You had me worried there for a minute," she said. Suddenly she turned, looking first at Cee Ten, then across at Sixer's charred form. "Are they—?"

"They won't bother us anymore," Janek said.

He retrieved Cee Ten's weapon. The droid had used up about a third of the clip during its last moments. Janek handed it to Kate.

"Don't be afraid to use it," he said. "If it's you or him, make sure you come out on top."

Kate managed a thin smile. "You want to rephrase that?"

Janek looked at her inquiringly. "Sorry?"

"Nothing, Janek, let's just get the hell out of here and find T.J."

The doors opened easily from the inside. There was no special code required. As the doors slid open, Janek pushed Kate to one side. The passage outside was empty, stretching silently into the distance.

Janek led the way at a run. His sole concern now was to reach Cade.

"Janek!" Kate yelled, and as he turned, he heard her pistol fire.

The elevator doors behind them had opened, and a trio of armed mercs had stepped into view. They were all carrying SMGs. Kate's shot caught one of them in the shoulder and spun him back inside the elevator. The others scattered, trying to bring their weapons to bear.

Janek picked the farthest man, triggered his pistol and sent a couple of steel-jackets into his chest. The merc flopped back against the wall, clawing for a handhold on its smooth surface as he slid to the floor.

The third attacker flipped up his SMG and opened up with a volley that missed Janek by a fraction. The stream of slugs shattered the glass wall behind him, blowing shards of glass in all directions. The continuous panel began to crack along its length. Whole sections started to fall inside the complex, more dropping away down the side of the building to the ground below. Alarm sirens began to wail, and warning lights flashed as the sanitized atmosphere became swiftly polluted by the outside air.

The merc stared in awe at what he'd done, realizing the implications of his actions. Janek found little to worry about on that score. With deliberate calm he leveled his autopistol and put the man out of his misery.

There was a scrabbling sound from inside the elevator. The wounded merc had regained his feet. Bracing himself against the door frame, he dragged his SMG into position, tracking in on Janek.

Kate had dropped to one knee, holding her pistol in both hands. She took aim and punched a slug through the merc's forehead. He was slammed back across the elevator car, crunching against the back wall.

"Keep this up and you could become dangerous," Janek said.

Kate ran forward and picked up two of the discarded SMGs. She tossed one to Janek, then took spare magazines from the dead merc's belt. Janek had done the same.

"Come on," he said. "That alarm is going to put everyone on their guard."

They reached the far end of the corridor. Janek accessed the airlock, and they waited as the heavy steel door opened. They entered the lock, and the door closed behind them. The outer lock opened with a soft hiss, and brilliant sunlight flooded the airlock. As Janek and Kate slipped out, a 4x4 swept into view. It came from the direction of the main building.

"Casull," Kate said as she recognized the man seated beside the driver.

Janek pushed her to one side, turning his SMG on the approaching 4x4. His shots shredded the front tires, throwing the 4x4 off course while the driver struggled to hold it level. Behind the windshield Jubal Casull was yelling and waving his arms. The driver stomped on the brakes, and the vehicle bounced to a hard stop. Casull kicked open his door and burst out of the truck. The robotics specialist carried a powerful-looking autorifle in his hands.

"What the hell have you done?" he screamed. "My building!"

He opened up, almost crying with rage. The cyborg's return fire raked the side of the 4x4, and the window glass in Casull's door exploded with a crackle, showering him with broken particles. The man ducked, his aim drifting away from Janek.

"Damn you, Janek! I wanted you to work with me. We could have done good things."

Janek didn't waste time on words. He laid a hard volley into Casull, punching the man back against the side of the vehicle. Blood burst through Casull's white suit. He sagged to his knees, oblivious to the pool of gasoline from the ruptured tank he was kneeling in. A groan of pain erupted from his thin lips. In an expression of pain and anger he smashed his left hand against the concrete, tearing the glove that covered his bionic hand. The exposed steel scraped across the rough sur-

face and generated a trail of sparks. There was a soft
thump of sound as the gasoline ignited. The burst of
flames swelled and grew in an instant, enveloping Casull in its fiery embrace. His clothing began to burn.
Casull stumbled back against the side of the truck, and
a high, shrill scream of agony issued from his lips. He
lost his balance and toppled facedown in the flames, his
body twisting and turning, soaking up more of the fuel.
When he did stagger to his feet, he was a walking ball
of flame. He lurched away from the blazing vehicle,
turning to where Janek stood. The hungry flames had
eaten away the syntho-flesh from his bionic limbs,
leaving his hands and arms exposed. The gleaming
metal shimmered in the consuming fire. He fell suddenly, his shriveling, steaming body arching once, then
relaxing as the fire burned deep into his very being.

Kate was frozen to the spot in horror. Janek took her
arm and led her away. He cut across the sloping lawns,
making for the main complex, aware that each passing
second lessened his chances of finding Cade. He just
hoped that his partner had managed to find or create his
own opportunity for escape.

11

They came face-to-face on the far side of the lawned area, where a natural hollow formed by the landscape offered temporary protection.

"T.J.!" Kate said, throwing herself into his arms for a brief moment of reconciliation.

Janek watched the embrace, then grunted. "You aren't going to indulge in that with me, are you?" he asked his partner.

"Not in your best fantasy," Cade said.

"Was I ever glad to hear that."

"Lukas Tane and his boys are on my tail," Cade said. "The sooner we quit this place the better."

"We need some transport," Kate pointed out.

"There it is," Janek said. He had been checking out the area.

Below them was a parking lot holding an assortment of freight and haulage vehicles belonging to the Amo-sin Corporation.

"Something like that would be handy for breaking out," Cade said.

They went down the long slope, reached the bottom and headed for the gate in the fence that surrounded the vehicle pool area.

There was a burly security droid at the gate.

"No point trying to talk our way past this one," Cade said.

He raised the SMG and fired through the droid's eyes. It fell back against the fence, emitting a shrill squeak of sound totally out of proportion to its size.

Janek swung into the cab of a huge tractor unit that was coupled to a massive silver gasoline tanker. By the time Cade and Kate had climbed in the other door, Janek had the powerful motor running.

"Hold on, folks," Janek yelled above the roar. He dropped the unit into gear and slammed his foot down hard on the gas pedal. The ponderous rig rolled forward out of the gate. Janek followed the marked drive that indicated the exit, ignoring the low-speed signs.

Bringing the rig around a long curve, Janek spotted the main gate ahead. The steel structure was already sliding shut.

"Over there," Kate said, pointing through the windshield.

Coming down a parallel drive were a couple of open-topped 4x4s. Each vehicle bristled with Lukas Tane's armed mercenaries.

"Go for it!" Cade yelled.

Janek stomped on the gas pedal. The tractor's powerful motor howled and the rig bulldozed forward, held steady by the cyborg's hands.

Muzzles flashed as the mercs opened fire, and bullets whacked the rig's steelwork.

Janek steered in the direction of the gates, ignoring the hostile fire.

The lead 4x4 swerved alongside as it surged onto the same section of the drive as the tanker. The gunfire increased, and bullets chewed away at the tractor's bodywork. The mercs were desperate to stop the rig from leaving Amosin's property.

Janek floored the gas pedal. As the rig increased speed, Janek eased the wheel around. The rig closed in on the 4x4. There was a tortured screech of tearing metal as the two vehicles became entangled. The coupling did nothing to stop the rig, but the 4x4 was battered mercilessly. The front end swung in, jamming between the tractor and the main tank. For a few yards it was carried along in the rig's headlong rush for the gates. One of its front tires burst, then the 4x4 flipped over. The tanker's double set of rear wheels bounced over the disintegrating vehicle, crushing metal and flesh in a blur of destruction.

Janek fought the bucking wheel, pulling the skidding rig back on line, and seconds later they hit the main gate. The ponderous, solid bulk of the rig, traveling at over sixty miles per hour, cut through the gates and ripped them from their supports. Tires squealed in protest as the rig bounced from side to side, and the rear wheels of the tanker were airborne for a while. Janek hung on to the spinning wheel, his immense strength the only thing that saved the rig from going totally out of control. He fought it for what seemed an eternity before the rig settled back on a straight course.

Then the cyborg took the feeder road that led them back to the main highway.

Kate flopped back in her seat, rubbing a badly bruised shoulder. She looked paler, and her eyes were big in her face. "Is his driving always like this?" she asked.

"Hell, no," Cade said. "This is one of his better days."

They barreled along Interstate 87, heading back toward New York. Cade checked the rearview mirror. He was hoping to see nothing but the normal traffic flow.

At first that was all he did see, but he kept his eyes glued to the mirror.

Suddenly he spotted one of the 4x4 open trucks weaving through the busy lanes.

"Damn!" he said.

"What is it?" Janek asked.

"This is getting to be like a crazy dream," Cade said. "We just keep jumping from one damn chase to another."

Janek laid his foot down hard. The rig surged forward, leaving the traffic far behind as they reached a long clear stretch of the interstate.

"We losing him?"

"No way," Cade said. "You can't outrun a 4x4 in a rig like this."

The cyborg scanned the mirror himself. The 4x4 was the only vehicle in sight now, locked on the rig's rear. Janek focused in on the occupants, and his enhanced vision allowed him to make out the hardware they were carrying.

"Okay, let's dump him," Janek said. "Here, take the wheel."

Cade slid behind the steering wheel. He held the rig on a steady course.

"Janek!" Kate called, and there was fear in her voice.

Glancing across the cab, Cade saw the cyborg opening the passenger door.

"Now what?"

"You just keep this thing on the road," Janek said over his shoulder, and vanished from sight.

Swinging around to the rear of the cab, Janek braced himself on the swaying platform. He knelt down and disconnected the flexible lines that delivered air and fluid to the tanker's braking and hydraulic systems. He freed the power cable, then took hold of the lock bar on the tanker's coupling to the tractor. He released the pressure and yanked the lever to the open position.

There was a moment's hesitation before the huge tanker slid free. The moment it cleared the rear of the tractor unit, the front of the tanker dropped to the ground, scoring deep into the surface of the interstate. A shower of fiery sparks leaped up from the tanker. It carried on for a couple of hundred yards, then began to turn. Twisting, then rolling, it toppled on its side. The forward momentum kept it moving as it turned broadside across the highway.

Above the screech of tortured metal, Janek picked up the shriek of locked tires burning the highway. As the bulk of the tanker swung around, he saw the 4x4 closing on it fast, then swerve as the wheelman tried to brake. There was no way he could avoid the massive object. The 4x4 caught the swinging end of the moving tanker and did a slow, full flip, landing upside down. The truck's impact burst a seam in the curving barrel, and gasoline flooded out in a long, glistening trail.

Janek caught the first gleam of flame as a spark ignited the vapor. The fire leaped back toward the tanker itself, and the whole thing suddenly became a moving fireball. The gas exploded with a sucking roar, throwing flame high into the sky. The boiling mass surged up and out, hungry tentacles reaching for the tractor. Cade slammed hard down on the throttle, sending the rig clear. He kept up speed for the next few miles, until the blazing wreck of the tanker was a speck. Then he eased off, giving Janek a chance to climb back inside the cab.

"That was beautifully underplayed," Cade remarked dryly as the cyborg dropped back in his seat.

"Don't embarrass me," Janek said.

"We've got to dump this thing soon," Cade said. "If Sinclair has cops on his payroll, they'll spot us easy."

"It'll be dark in a couple of hours," Janek said. "If we can hide out somewhere until then, maybe they'll miss us."

A few miles later they spotted a dirt road. Cade rolled the tractor along it, pushing through the overhanging foliage that bordered the narrow track. He backed the rig deep in a stand of trees and cut the motor.

"A day out with you guys can never be called dull," Kate said as they climbed out of the rig.

"You okay?" Cade asked.

"Scared out of my pants," she replied. "Apart from that, I'm fine."

They stretched their limbs, then sat in the shade of the rig.

Janek glanced skyward, raising a hand.

"Hear something?" Cade asked.

The cyborg nodded, turning his head slowly as he scanned the sky.

"Chopper," he said.

The helicopter appeared as a small dark speck, high up, flying level with the highway. When Cade and Kate finally picked it up, they saw it losing altitude. It flashed by them, staying with the highway as it kept up its search.

"Persistent bunch," Cade observed. "Keep watching, partner, they could be back."

Cade laid his SMG on the ground.

"Time we checked the hardware."

Between them they had two handguns and three heavier weapons. Ammunition was sparse.

"And this," Cade said.

He took the dictopad from his pocket and held it up.

"Casull was making notes while Sinclair was speaking on the phone," he explained. "When he took off, he left it behind."

Kate took it and pressed the keypad. The pad began to disgorge a sheet of paper, transferring the text from its memory into a hard copy. She scanned the sheet, then passed it to Cade.

"You want to read this."

Cade started to examine the text, but Janek was crowding him. "Well," he said impatiently. "Can we all have a look, Thomas?"

He practically snatched the sheet from Cade. He absorbed the information quickly and gave a chuckle of pleasure.

"Why do humans feel this need to write everything down, T.J.? Names. Times. Places."

"Because we don't have computers for brains," Cade said.

"I resent that," Janek snapped. "Computer! You'll be wanting to switch me off at night next."

"That list isn't going to make things easier," Cade said. "Sinclair is going to realize it's missing, and he'll assume we have it. So everybody involved is going to tighten up. If we reckoned to have it tough before, just see what happens now."

"Let's figure this out," Janek said. "Sinclair's operation hinges on his people getting control of Skylance. That's where the military comes in. They provide a substitute crew when the monthly swap takes place. Sinclair's people are put on board Skylance and take over. Once that happens, Sinclair can make his intentions known to the White House. His insiders in the police department control local resistance in the city, and his people in the mayor's office are ready to step in

to handle the administration side. New York and
Washington are major admin areas for the eastern sea-
board. His media contacts will push out the don't-panic
messages. If Sinclair gets control of both areas, he's in
a strong position."

"The names in the second half of the text," Kate remarked, "I recognize some of them as media people or
bureaucrats, and other highly placed people in the police department in Washington."

"Duplicates of the New York listing," Cade said.
"Sinclair has this all worked out."

"So how do we bust it wide open?"

"We'll have to improvise some. We can't risk talking
to many people because we don't know who might be
on Sinclair's team. The names on the list may be key
players. But he could have others keeping a low profile."

"T.J., we're only three people," Kate said.

"We need our own backup," Cade admitted. "And
I think I know where we can get some."

THE ROADSIDE DINER had just put on its lights as Cade
stepped inside. The place was quiet. Just two other
customers were present, already busy with their meals.

A service droid, wearing grease-stained whites, came
to take Cade's order.

"All I need is the phone right now," Cade said. "Car
broke down."

The droid indicated the booth at the far end of the
diner.

Cade settled on the stool and picked up the handset.
He punched in a number sequence that would give him
direct access to Milt Schuberg's office, hoping that the
NYPD cop was in.

"What's happening?" Schuberg asked the moment he recognized Cade's face on the vid-screen. "Right about now you're rated most-wanted number one."

"Can you get out of the office and call me on a public line?"

Schuberg nodded. He wrote down the number Cade gave him and cut the connection. The next few minutes were the longest Cade had ever lived. He expected to hear police sirens any second.

The vid-phone rang, and he snatched up the handset. The screen fuzzed over, then cleared to show Schuberg's sweating face.

"Jesus, T.J., don't make me run like that ever again."

"You'll thank me when you're fit," Cade said. "Favor time, buddy. I'm collecting every one the NYPD owes me today."

Schuberg realized Cade was in deadly earnest. "Shoot. You got it, T.J."

"I need you to get a team together, Milt. Men you know you can trust. And no mistakes. Pick the wrong guys, and we're all dead."

"To put it mildly, what the fuck is going on?"

"The worst thing you could imagine."

"Christ, don't tell me the Yankees are going to throw the league final."

"There's going to be an attempt to take over the government, and we're smack in the middle."

"Hell, T.J., why is it you who always gets mixed up in this kind of thing? Why not a nice juicy mass murder? No, you always go for the big ones."

"Lucky I guess. Milt, we're short on time. This has to be done tonight."

"Give me a minute…okay, listen. You remember the old place in Queens?"

At Cade's nod, Schuberg went on. "Give me one hour and meet me there. I got to do some calling first."

"One more thing. Be careful who you deal with." Cade read out the names on his list. "They're on the other team. There might be others we don't know about."

"Jesus, do you realize you got the chief of police down as one of the bad guys?"

"Makes you see how they've been able to keep tabs on me, Milt. So watch yourself."

"Don't worry. The kind of guys I hang about with ain't got the sense to come in out of the rain—but they're honest cops."

"And Milt, could you pick up some fresh clothes for Janek and me? Anything. The rags we're in now a blind man could spot. Spare handguns and holsters if you can lay your hands on them."

"Boy, are you ever going to owe me, pal," Schuberg crowed.

Cade hung up the phone and left the diner, his stomach growling at the rich aroma of brewing coffee. He crossed to where Janek and Kate were waiting.

"Milt's with us," Cade said. "He's going to round up some of his buddies and join us at his old place out in Queens."

"How do we get there?" Janek asked. "Thumb a ride?"

"You're a cop," Cade said. "Improvise."

"I guess stealing *two* vehicles in one day can't get me in any deeper," Janek muttered ungraciously.

He strolled across the parking lot and examined the cars parked there. The best of the bunch was a six-month-old Dodge Lunar. Janek checked the driver's door and found it unlocked. He slipped behind the wheel and reached under the dash to locate the ignition microcircuit. In less than thirty seconds the light came on and the motor burst into life. Kate climbed into the back and stretched out across the seat.

"Head for Queens," Cade said, closing the passenger door.

Janek rolled the Dodge quietly out of the lot and onto the highway, flicking on the lights once he had the car out of sight of the diner.

Turning on the radio, Cade punched through the stations, hoping to pick up any news items. He heard nothing out of the ordinary. No mention of anything to do with Amosin or the involvement of the Justice Department. Someone was going to a lot of trouble to keep things on an ordinary, everyday level. The public was being kept unaware of anything unusual going on. By the time they did hear anything, it would all be over— if Sinclair and his people had their way.

"Hey, leave that," Janek insisted as a local jazz station filled the car with music.

Cade opened the dash compartment and rifled through it. He found a crumpled pack of cigars and a few dollar bills. Settling back in the seat, he lit one of the cigars.

"One of the good things about the last couple of days, Thomas, is you not having time to smoke," Janek said.

Cade inhaled the rich smoke. "It was worth the wait," he replied in tones of reverence.

"You really think so?"

"First diner you see, pull in so I can pick up some food and coffee for Kate and me."

"Can't you go without? Anyway, Kate's asleep. She must be worn-out."

"For coffee I'm awake," Kate mumbled from the backseat.

"Cigars. Coffee. Can't you two do anything except stuff things into your bodies?"

"Remind me to explain the significance of that last remark to him," Cade said.

"I don't think he could grasp the concept," Kate said.

"I'm teamed up with a couple of perverts," Janek grumbled. "And I'm supposed to save the world with help like this?"

12

The houses on the street hadn't changed in design or construction over the years. The new century had almost passed this section of Astoria by. The rows of clapboard houses defied the new age, as did the closeness of the community. Milt Schuberg's place was no different. It had been in his family for three generations and had passed to Schuberg with the death of his father. He used the place for weekend breaks, intending to retire there when his hitch with the NYPD was up.

Cade eased onto the street. By the light of the streetlights he could see a number of vehicles on the sloping drive of Schuberg's house.

"Looks quiet enough," Janek said.

Cade drove by the house, reached the end of the street and turned around. He parked behind a dusty car and cut the motor, sitting in the darkness while he checked the house and the surrounding area.

Opening his door, Cade stepped out, the SMG in his hands. The neighborhood lay quiet and calm. He could hear the soft sound of music coming from an open window across the street. There was nothing to suggest a setup, with hostile guns aimed at them. Past experience had taught Cade to be aware of unnatural situations. Stakeouts, despite attempting to present normal life, tended to have a quieting effect on the neutralized zone. A strained, hard-edged hollowness. There was no feeling like that here.

"Let's go," Cade said.

As he led the way up to the house, Kate followed while Janek trailed slightly behind and kept an eye on the street. As they reached the front door, it opened and Milt Schuberg stood there.

"Cautious as ever, T.J.," he said as they filed in. Schuberg closed the door and led them through to the living room.

Cade recognized every man in the room. There were seven of them, all long-serving cops who had come up off the streets, like Schuberg. Grizzled, hard street cops who knew right from wrong and still believed in the old values.

They sat and listened as Cade outlined the situation and the way he expected things to go. He made no attempt to cover up the fact that there were cops in the department who had sold out, including the NYPD chief of police. He revealed their names and included the others in the conspiracy from the city administration and the media.

"The way we've timetabled this thing," he concluded, "they'll be making their move tonight. The new crew for Skylance shuttles up in the early hours of this morning. I'd guess by now Sinclair's people will have made their move. Nothing we can do about that. Our best chance is to hit them after the takeover. They'll be feeling pretty confident by then.

"We'll get one chance to turn this thing around. If we can hit them when they least expect it, the odds are with us."

"No guarantees," Janek said. "Any mistakes will get you killed."

"Hell, I've been working under those rules ever since I pinned on my badge," Schuberg said.

"That's it," Cade said. "I need your help on this one, fellers."

The silence lasted all of five seconds.

Ed MacNamara, a veteran of the NYPD with as many years as Schuberg, was the first man to speak up. "Cade, when something makes *you* itch, it has to be true. You got my vote."

"I don't always approve of the way you play," said Hernandez, a member of the narcotics division, "but I trust your word. And I can bring in at least a dozen more who are loyal."

The others followed with their own brief words of acceptance. They were aware of the price of failure, but it was something that had to be done, albeit unofficially.

"I'll leave the details to you," Cade said. "Pick your targets and get your people in position. Be ready to move when you hear from me or Janek."

A burly homicide sergeant named Kluge asked, "What's your part in this, Cade?"

"The crew on Skylance has to be put on ice. As long as Sinclair controls the satellite, he's got the winning hand." Cade glanced at Janek. "That's our job."

"I just knew he was going to say that," Janek whispered to Kate. "Always has to do it the hard way."

Kluge didn't ask anything more. He'd made up his mind long ago that Cade was a man who knew what he was doing and was willing to put his life on the line to do it. This time around Kluge didn't envy the Justice cop his chosen task, but he admired Cade's courage in accepting the gamble.

"Getting Skylance back won't stop Sinclair completely," Cade said. "If we do regain control, we keep the news to ourselves. I want to hit Sinclair and his people while he still believes he has the edge. We allow him any slack, he'll use it to cover his tracks and maybe even walk away free and clear. I don't want to give him that chance."

"T.J., you want to tie this down? Let's have names and places so we can pick our teams and assign specific tasks," Schuberg said. "I'll get some coffee on the stove."

"All right, and I'll keep track," Kate said. "You guys need an objective opinion."

Cade picked up the bag holding the clothes Schuberg had brought along for him and Janek.

"Give me a chance to get cleaned up and into a fresh shirt and we'll talk."

THIRTY MINUTES LATER they were dispersing, leaving only Milt Schuberg with Cade, Janek and Kate.

"They'll do it if anyone can, T.J.," Schuberg said.

"Milt, I want you to take care of Kate," Cade said.

He saw the protest rise in her eyes. "Let me do something," she said.

"Kate, I don't want you being taking hostage and used in negotiations. So how about getting all this down for publication?" Cade suggested. "Use the tape George sent you. Casull's dictopad. Everything you've seen and heard. Every name and location. All the stuff Janek pulled from the computer banks. The full story. Hard facts, Kate. If we luck out, you'll have that to push through every news agency you can think of."

"Leave that to me," Schuberg said. "I can fix up a place for her. Get what she needs and provide protection."

"I can take care of myself," Kate said with annoyance. "I can even shoot straight—Janek will tell you that. So don't patronize me. But when you get back, T.J., we're taking a break. Somewhere nice. I'm getting worried about you. Chasing about. Getting into trouble all the time."

"Blame him," Cade said, jerking a thumb in Janek's direction.

"Why me?" Janek protested.

"Because he's got to have his excuses," Kate said angrily. "He thinks he's the only cop around who can save the damn world. The only one who has to put his neck on the block. Well, you're not, Thomas Jefferson Cade, and it's time you realized there are people who...who..."

"Who...?" Cade asked casually.

"That's not fair," Janek said. "You're making it hard for Kate."

"Yeah," Schuberg said, "he's right, T.J. Don't be a jerk. Can't you see she's trying to say she loves you. Jesus, even I can figure that out."

Cade felt angry at himself. He'd been trying to keep the moment light, and there was Kate doing the opposite. And he had put his clumsy foot right in it, as usual.

"Aw, Kate, I can't get all choked up now." Cade drew her to him. "We'll do what you said. Get away for a while. Give ourselves a chance to sort things out."

"Yeah," Schuberg said. "Hey, you can leave old tin pants with me."

"No way," Janek protested. "I can look after myself."

They climbed into the car, Janek taking the wheel.

"Newark," Cade said. "The shuttle port."

THE NEWARK SHUTTLE PORT was all but deserted at 3:30 a.m. Janek had parked the car in one of the near-empty lots.

Under their jackets the Justice cops wore shoulder rigs holding the autopistols Schuberg had supplied. The SMGs were left in the trunk of the car.

Cade led the way to the terminal building. The glass doors slid open at their approach, and they stepped inside the brightly lit terminal.

Soft music filtered through concealed speakers. A row of TV booths played to nonexistent viewers. Even at this hour the eternal commercial barrage still persisted. A chrometal service droid paused in its labors to stare at one of the screens, resting on the handle of the vacu-mop it had been cleaning the floor with.

Cade made his way to a ticket counter. The clerk on duty smiled brightly. Chestnut-colored hair framed flawless features as the clerk smiled at him. The perfection of face and form, as well as something too even about her manner, let Cade know that she was a cyborg.

"May I help you, sir?"

"I need to hire a shuttle to get up to Pegasus-2."

"Certainly, sir. How soon do you require departure?"

"Straight away," Cade said.

"Cash or credit?"

"It'll have to be credit," Cade said, and took out his card.

"Thank you, sir. I won't be a moment."

The cyborg ran the card through the machine. It registered and the credit limit showed up on the monitor. Cade could have told her it would be valid. The card was a Justice Department special, issued to all marshals..Each card was given a different name so that covers could be maintained if required.

"Everything seems to be in order, sir."

The clerk typed in particulars, and a sign-out sheet slid from the slot of the com unit. Cade signed on the line. Picking up her telephone, the clerk called the shuttle facility and ordered Cade's ship.

"Your shuttle will be ready in approximately ten minutes, sir. If you would like to wait over there, I'll give you a call."

Cade rejoined Janek. "Ten minutes," he said.

"If we live that long," Janek told him, looking very nonchalant, but his tone alerted Cade.

"Two guys came in a minute ago. They're over at the vending machines. I recognized one of them from our time at Amosin. One of Tane's mercs. I expect the other is, as well."

"Well, Sinclair has made us some kind of priority, I guess . . . just to cover all the bases. He'll figure if we've worked out what he's doing, we'll try and stop him."

"Those two haven't done anything yet," Janek said. "No communication with anybody. Probably they want to see if we're alone before they make a move."

"Let's deal with them before they do," Cade said.

He broke away and headed for the bank of vidphones on the far side of the terminal. Janek turned in the other direction and made for the up-ramp leading to the terminal's lounge area.

Tane's men separated and followed.

Janek reached the top of the ramp and quickly
stepped into the shadow of a massive support column
at the entrance to the silent, deserted lounge. He picked
up the sound of the approaching merc. The man had
pulled a squat, matt black autopistol and was trying to
walk lightly, holding it down at his side. As he reached
the head of the ramp, he paused, staring into the gloom
of the empty lounge, and realized he'd walked into a
setup.

Janek leaned out from behind the column, striking
with blinding speed. His right hand grasped the merc's
gunhand, squeezing hard and crushing the fingers into
the metal of the pistol. As the merc's mouth opened to
let out a cry of pain, Janek punched him full in the face
with his left fist. The man's head rocked back from the
power of the blow. His neck snapped, and blood gushed
from his crushed nose and lips. His legs buckled and he
sagged to the carpeted floor. Janek dragged him across
the lounge and dumped him behind the bar, then took
the man's gun and searched him for any other weapons. Apart from a spare magazine, he found nothing.
The man was clean. No ID. Just a few coins for the
telephone.

Janek returned to the terminal floor. He saw that
Cade was still at the vid-phone booths. The merc who
had trailed him was also there. From where Janek was
standing, it looked as if they were having a friendly
conversation.

It might have been a conversation, he decided, but it
would be far from friendly.

As he moved closer, he picked up the merc's voice.

"It's already gone down. No way you can stop it."

"We can make certain you don't earn your bonus," Janek said gently. He held up the gun he'd taken from the dead man.

The man's eyes widened perceptibly. "What did you do with Rico?"

"I snapped his neck," Janek said. "You want to see how?"

"Killing me won't change a thing," the merc said defiantly.

"It'll get my day off to a good start," Cade told him. "Unless you can persuade me with something better."

"Like what?"

"How about a few names?"

"Names? What is this, a charade? What the hell you talkin' about, Cade?"

Janek looked inquiringly at his partner, and Cade flashed him a grin. "I'll tell you later."

He left the merc with Janek and crossed to the ticket counter.

"How's my shuttle doing?" he asked.

The clerk checked on the monitor. "You can go through now, and you can board in a few minutes." The cybo gave him a flawless smile and handed over the authorization docket and launch pass. "Bay nine."

They walked through to the transit tunnel and the moving strip that took them to the launch-bay access terminal. A droid took the paperwork and checked it, then directed them along the correct tunnel. At the end of the brightly lit tunnel, with its Muzak and vidscreens, a large holographic display instructed them on the delights of the Pegasus-2 orbiting platform.

"Where are you taking me?" the merc asked as Janek walked him down the final tunnel to the embarkation bay.

"Trip of a lifetime," Janek told him. "You might like it so much you won't want to come back."

"No way you're getting me on any shuttle," the merc protested. "You want to hear someone yell, you just try."

"I had a feeling you were going to be trouble," Janek said. "So we do it the hard way, Jack."

"What hard way? And my name ain't Jack."

"I don't care what it is," Janek said, taking out his marshal's badge and hooking it to the top pocket of his jacket. He pulled his autopistol and jammed it against the merc's side, while his fingers gripped the man's left arm with the force of a closing vice. "You remember one thing, Jack. We're Justice marshals. That means we get to do things nobody else can. I could shoot you now and justify it. You'd be dead, so either way you lose. Think about it."

Cade pulled his own badge. He'd hoped they could get on board the shuttle without the need to expose themselves, but he could live with the heat if need be.

The droid at the embarkation bay had a security guard with him. The guy was armed and had a look on his face that told Cade he wasn't best pleased at having to leave his office before daybreak.

"Officer," Cade said, deciding to take the lead. "Sorry you had to be dragged out this early. I'm Marshal Cade. My partner, Marshal Janek. We're from the Justice Department. We have to get this prisoner up to Pegasus-2. He's going on a long vacation, for four years, in fact. Hard labor."

"What he do?" the guard asked.

"Killed some police officers during a drug bust," Janek said. "Left his partners to shoot it out while he ran. He's a very unpopular guy. That right, Jack?"

The droid methodically processed the paperwork, ignoring the conversation going on around it.

"Son of a bitch," the guard said. He eyed the merc. "He looks a mean mother, too."

"You said it, Officer," Janek responded. "This guy is so doped up, he doesn't really need the shuttle. If you know what I mean."

The merc strained against the cyborg's tight grip on his arm.

"No way I'm goin' in that shuttle. Look, Officer, these fuckers want to kill me. They already threatened me."

"See what I mean?" Janek said. "To be honest, Officer, I'll be glad when we get him off our hands. Let the security people handle him."

"Your papers are all in order," the droid said, handing them back to Cade.

The security man stepped back and opened the sliding door.

"Good luck," he said as Cade and Janek ushered their prisoner through. The door slid shut with a soft thump.

Cade boarded the shuttle and checked it out while Janek dumped the merc in one of the launch couches and used the safety belts to secure him. Returning from closing the hatch, Cade bent over the merc.

"While we take off, I want you to consider your options. Play games with me, and I'll shoot you out of the garbage disposal tube once we hit orbit. Give me what I want, and you could walk and take your chances with the cops. Right now I'm up against it, so I don't have too much to lose. That means I'm prepared to forget this badge I'm wearing and do it the hard way. Your choice."

Janek took the controls, coasting out to the launch pad. He locked on to the autoramp, allowing the computer-controlled launching sequence to initiate takeoff. As the shuttle was brought up to launch thrust, he ran an instrument and control check. Satisfied, he settled in his padded seat and waited.

The shuttle reached thrust speed. As the powerful engines kicked back into the scorched blast pit, the sleek shuttle burst free from the angled ramp and curved up into the gray, dawning sky. After two minutes the autosignal passed control over to Janek, and he keyed in their course. Normally he would have enjoyed flying the shuttle manually, but he had other things to attend to.

"Thinking time's over, Jack," he said, standing over the strapped-down merc.

"The name's Curtis, for Christ's sake. Lon Curtis. Now what the hell are you bastards playing at?"

13

"Skylance. Skylance, answer me, Bridger. I know you're there. Don't fuck about. This is Curtis. Lon Curtis. Pick up the damn phone and speak to me!"

The vid-screen remained blank.

"Don't play dumb with me, Bridger. I ain't got the patience. Just talk to me, man. Stop playin' with your new fuckin' toy and talk to me."

The screen fuzzed, then cleared to show the head and shoulders of a man dressed in a pressure suit.

"Took your time, didn't you, Bridger?" Curtis snapped.

"The hell it is you, Curtis."

"Who do you think it was—Buck Rogers?"

"You in that shuttle floating around outside?" Bridger asked.

"No, dumb-ass. I'm tap-dancing on the fuckin' hull. Now shut up and listen.

"Rico and me got the shuttle port assignment. Cade and that Cybo partner showed up and took a shuttle up to Pegasus-2. We followed them up there and managed to get the drop on them, but not before they offed Rico. I got them back on a shuttle to bring back down, only the cybo went crazy on me. Said if he couldn't get you guys alive, he'd ram you with the shuttle. Set the damn shuttle on a collision course with Skylance and put the motors on full burn. I had to blow him away to stop him. Only now I ain't got enough juice in this damn thing to take me back down. Get me on board, Bridger.

I don't like these shuttles. I got one dead cybo, and
Cade strapped down in a chair. Pull me in, pal, and I'll
give you Rico's half of the bonus old man Sinclair
promised for whoever delivers Cade."

"Let me see him, Lon," Bridger demanded.

Curtis moved away from the vid-screen, pressing the
button that opened the lens setting. The expanding picture showed Cade strapped down in one of the launch
seats and Janek sprawled on the deck of the shuttle.

"Okay?" Curtis asked. "You want a souvenir tape
of it all?"

"Half the bonus?" Bridger asked.

"Yeah."

"Can you get that shuttle to the docking bay?"
Bridger asked.

"I'll manage it."

Bridger nodded. "I'll get the defense shield dropped
for you. Don't want my investment blowing away, do
I?" he said, and broke the connection.

"You did that like you practiced all your life," Janek said. He stood up and moved to unstrap Cade.

"With a gun at my back, what choice did I have?"
Curtis asked sullenly.

Janek looked down at the autopistol he held. The vid-
screen hadn't shown the weapon directed at Curtis.

"I forgot I had this."

"Yeah," Curtis said. "And you wouldn't dump me
out the garbage chute, either? Now what?"

"We go and join your buddies," Cade said, "as soon
as you get the all clear."

"If you expect them to quit without a fight, you're
crazy," Curtis said.

"That's up to them," Cade told the merc. "Seeing
you reminded me, Curtis. I haven't changed my mind.

Cross me, and I will dump you. I haven't got a lot of affection for you and your buddies. Six men dead down below so your bogus crew can get on the shuttle. Another six dead on Skylance. How many more if Sinclair's blackmail doesn't work?''

During the flight up to Pegasus-2, then the two-hour diversion to bring them within sight of Skylance and its ring of defense satellites, Lon Curtis had given Cade a lot of information. The merc didn't like space travel. It unsettled him, made him vulnerable, and he'd been willing to talk. Partly to make a deal for himself, partly to take his mind off where he was.

The merc had admitted that the original changeover crew had been killed when the bogus crew had taken over. The same fate had been decided for the Skylance crew. Sinclair had decided on a total wipeout to avoid the chance of any resistance. Sinclair's creed dictated that those against him were to be removed without the least hesitation. The killing had started with the three Amosin employees the moment they had shown a change of heart and wanted out of the conspiracy. It had only been George Takagi's bad luck that he had stumbled across the reports of their deaths, decreeing that he had to die himself. Once Takagi had been dealt with, the ball had been kept rolling. As far as Sinclair was concerned, there was no turning back. It was total commitment to the cause—for everyone.

Curtis had no answer to Cade's anger. The deal that had sounded so worthwhile and held the promise of vast profits paled when he thought how easily he might end up dead himself.

An audible warning sounded, followed by a metallic voice. ''Shuttle, you may approach and dock. The shield is down.''

Janek took the controls and eased the shuttle over Skylance. The orbiting weapons platform dwarfed the shuttle. The huge weapon pods, slung beneath the disklike upper shell of the platform, held an array of awesome technology. Nuclear missiles capable of encircling the globe and striking with pinpoint accuracy were backed up by a series of laser weapons that could reach far into space, as well as seek out any designated point on Earth. Skylance also boasted a range of particle-beam weapons far in advance of any other systems in existence. A breakthrough in the particle-beam research program had allowed the U.S. to gain years of advantage over the rest of the world, and it had been decided to optimize that breakthrough by planting the weapons on Skylance. Despite its awesome size and destructive potential, the satellite's design allowed it to be manned by a six-man crew, assisted by a team of techdroids.

Making a couple of false attempts, Janek locked on to the platform's docking bay on the third try. As the shuttle eased into position, the sound of the electroclamps making contact rang through the hull of the shuttle.

"Move, Curtis," Janek said.

"Where we going?" the merc demanded.

"We can't have you in the way," Cade said. "Put him in the aft locker, Janek."

"You bastards!" Curtis began. "Locker, my ass. You're dumping me through the garbage chute!"

The light on the access hatch set in the deck flashed green. It meant that the hatch could now be opened.

Cade turned without warning, his fist arcing around to connect with Curtis's jaw. The man's eyes rolled up in his head, and he slumped to the floor. Janek grabbed him and bundled him out of sight. He was back in a short time, having locked the merc in a storage locker.

"He can yell all he wants. No one can hear."

"You set?" Cade asked. "We don't open that hatch, they're going to get suspicious."

Janek nodded. He keyed in the sequence, and they stood back as the hatch released and began to open. It was a slow process, the heavy metal sliding back to reveal the short access tunnel that led down into Skylance.

Though the Justice cops were expecting to see one of Sinclair's crew to show himself, they didn't anticipate his reaction as he shoved his head and shoulders through the hatch.

He took one look and started yelling.

A fraction of a second later he started shooting.

Janek shouldered Cade aside, dropped to one knee and returned fire. He felt a bullet pound his left shoulder. The cyborg rocked back on his heels, absorbing the impact. Then he triggered his own weapon, and the soft-nosed hollowpoints whacked into the merc's skull. The dying merc lost his grip on the hatch and tumbled back down the ladder. He crashed down on the metal deck, spilling blood across the walkway.

The moment he'd fired, Janek went through the hatch. He slid down the ladder, stepped over the dead merc and pounded along the walkway. The cyborg had a singular purpose. He wanted to reach the communications center before a message could be sent out to Sinclair's base informing them that Skylance was under attack. At the end of the walkway, he located a com unit and keyed in a location search. The screen obliged, showing an illustrated route from where Janek was to the communications center. The cyborg memorized the route. If he wasn't interfered with, it would take him just under one minute to reach the place.

He sprinted along the uniformly similar passageways. The only differentiating characteristics were the color stripes on the bulkheads, showing the exact location of each block. Janek watched them alter as he moved from section to section—red to blue to orange to green.

Green was the communications center.

As Janek reached the hatchway leading into the center, he was confronted by one of Lukas Tane's combat droids barring his way.

"You got an entry code?" it demanded with a definite sneer in its voice.

"You want an entry code? Have one," Janek said, and jammed the muzzle of his autopistol against one of the droid's eyes and blew its electronic brain out the back of its skull.

As the droid clattered to the deck, Janek moved by.

The center had only one occupant. He was leaning across his communications desk and frantically yelling into a phone, twisting his head as he heard the sound of the shot.

"Assistance needed . . . right now . . ."

The mercenary soldier dropped the phone and snatched up his SMG. The weapon crackled harshly, sending slugs clanging into the bulkhead close to where Janek had been standing.

The cyborg had already moved, lunging to the right as the merc let fly. He let himself fall, his gunhand outstretched. He slithered along the deck plates, hearing the merc curse as he kicked his chair back on its flexible stalk to give himself room to operate.

Janek wasn't allowed that luxury. Propped up on one hand, he tracked in on the merc and punched out a trio of close-spaced shots. They caught the merc in the upper chest, kicking him back across the desk and onto the deck. The front of the merc's white pressure suit glistened with blood that pumped from his wounds.

Already on his feet, Janek punched the button that closed the center's hatch. Having secured the place, Janek crossed to the communications desk and studied the layout. It was a familiar setup. From here he could control the whole communications network throughout the platform, and also maintain radio silence if he wanted. Nothing could go out from Skylance now except through Janek.

The first thing he did was cut the transmission facility from the weapons center, isolating them from the outside world. If they wanted to speak to Sinclair, they would have to get by him first.

DROPPING DOWN beside the dead merc, Cade snatched up the man's discarded handgun and jammed it in his belt. He might need the extra firepower.

Cade forgot about the communications center. Janek would handle that. Cade's own objective was the weapons control center. He had to get that out of the hands of Sinclair's crew.

Until they were all taken care of, the possibility of their actually using Skylance's weapons systems still posed a threat. Knowing the way the human mind worked, Cade accepted that the mercs might use the weapons out of pure bloody-mindedness.

He paused at a com unit and asked for a location. The designated route led across to the center of the

platform, from where he would have to drop down two
levels.

He made it to the elevator shaft he'd seen on the route
without resistance.

As he entered the circular area that housed the elevator bank, a weapon opened up off to his right. Cade
felt a burning sting across his right upper arm. Instead
of ducking for cover, he took a chance and threw himself forward. The hidden gunner hadn't expected such
a move. He had started to relocate, and Cade caught
him in the open. The merc's submachine gun was lowered. Before he could lift it, Cade took him out with a
single shot that caught him between the eyes. The merc
took an uncertain step backward, slamming up against
the bulkhead, then slithered to the deck. A thin ribbon
of blood trickled out of the dark hole in his forehead,
but it was nothing compared to the dark, sticky mess
that was plastered to the bulkhead behind him.

Cade hit the elevator button, keeping his eyes on the
indicator panel as it rose to his floor. He stepped to the
side as the door slid open. Glancing across the opening, he checked the floor of the elevator. Unless there
was someone perched halfway up the side of the car, the
elevator was empty.

Cade entered the car and punched in the level he
wanted. As the elevator dropped, Cade took evasive
action himself in case someone was waiting for him. He
used the barrel of the autopistol to knock out the car's
lights, plunging him into blackness. It wasn't much, but
at least it might give him a couple of seconds when the
elevator stopped.

He felt it slowing. Pressing against the side, Cade
waited as the car stopped. The doors seemed to take an
eternity before they opened. Cade stayed where he was,

caution dictating his movements. His decision to hold back paid off when he heard a faint movement outside the elevator. The sound repeated itself seconds later.

Gripping the autopistol in both hands, he eased around the edge of the door, the muzzle seeking its target.

A maintenance droid stood a few feet away from the elevator. It turned its head as Cade stepped out.

"There appears to be a malfunction in the lighting system," it observed.

Cade lowered the handgun. "You want to fix it?" he said, and walked on by, leaving the droid peering into the dark interior of the car.

The color coding on the bulkheads told him he was nearing the weapons center. Stepping through an open hatch, he recognized the purple color he wanted. The bulkhead also bore the symbols for weapons. Warning signs began to appear, indicating he was in a sensitive area. Cade noticed monitor cameras following his progress. Hopefully they would be transmitting to the communications center. If Janek was in control now, he would be able to stop the cameras transmitting to the weapons center and advertising his approach.

If the remaining crew were in the weapons center, it was possible they might be getting concerned. They had to know intruders were on the platform. If Janek had cut audio and visual communications, they could be getting jittery. And that could mean they might turn unpredictable.

The hatch to the weapons center blocked his way. It was closed. Cade checked the access panel next to it. The key panel held a triple row of buttons. There was no way he was going to break any code. If anyone could do that, it would have to be Janek.

Cade checked the bulkhead for a com unit. If he could speak to Janek, the cyborg might solve his problem. His luck held, and he found a com unit only yards from the hatchway. Keying in the advised number for the communications center, Cade crossed his fingers and hoped Janek was listening in.

"Janek, you there? Come on, answer me. This is T.J. We've got a problem."

The unit's vid-screen flashed, and Janek's face peered at Cade. "How's it going?"

"I'm at the weapons center. The hatch is secured. And this isn't one of those doors you break down with your shoulder, either."

"You'd better come to the communications center. We need to talk."

"On my way," Cade said. "Hey, are we okay to talk on this thing?"

Janek nodded. "I've got everything locked down. They only hear what I want them to hear."

"I wonder if there's any way to lock down the weapons, as well," Cade muttered to himself as he turned from the com unit. To his surprise, he got an answer.

"That can only be done from inside the center itself."

Cade whirled around, his gun lifting as he located the speaker.

"I'm not hostile," the tall cyborg said gently. "In fact, I'm on your side. I want these invaders off Skylance as much as you do."

Cade noticed the blue-and-gold badge stitched into the cybo's white jumpsuit. Above the Skylance emblem were the words Security Section—Officer Teclan.

"If you're that hot on dumping this bunch, how come they allowed you to walk around free?" Cade asked, still keeping his weapon trained on the cyborg.

Teclan smiled. "A fair question. When they hit, my human partner told me to lose myself in case there was a takeover. I did as he suggested. Skylance is a large platform, and I know every corner. I could hide from these people for as long as I wanted. I'd been in hiding for a while when I started to worry about my partner. I also realized I wasn't contributing too much, so I decided it was time to do what I'm supposed to. It appears you arrived at around that time, too."

"Your crew has probably been taken out," Cade said. "The way we see it, this hit squad isn't taking prisoners."

Teclan nodded in understanding. "I've already found that out," he said. "They're all dead. My partner included. What's behind it?"

"Gaining control of Skylance is part of a wider conspiracy. Fronted by a guy called Sinclair, who figures he could run the country better than the government."

"Where do you come in?"

Cade flashed his badge. "Justice Department. My partner, Janek, is in the communications center. We shut the place down so the mercs in the weapons center can't speak to their ground support."

"How many have you dealt with?"

"Two I can guarantee," Cade said. "Plus however many Janek's taken care of. Let's go find out."

"A number of combat droids came aboard with the bogus crew," Teclan said. "Did you know that?"

"No," Cade admitted. "Thanks for the information. How about your droids?"

"They're all noncombatant. Tech-droids. Service droids. I'm the only one programmed to take direct action in the event."

"Great," Cade said. "Janek's going to love you."

"THERE IS AN EMERGENCY airlock that accesses the weapons center," Teclan explained. "It can get us inside. The main power section is situated next to the lock for emergency shutoff. If we cut that power, there's no way they can activate any of the weapons."

"That's our way in," Cade said.

"Not so easy. The only way to reach the airlock is by walking across the outside of the platform."

Janek glanced at Cade, allowing a knowing smile to creep onto his lips.

"No problem," he said. "We can do it, Teclan."

"Hey, wait a damn minute..." Cade began.

"Makes sense, T.J.," the cyborg explained. "If you go, it means finding a suit and getting you all the hardware. All Teclan and I need are magno-boots, and we're ready. Face it, T.J., we're better suited to this than you are."

"He is right, Marshal Cade," Teclan agreed.

"Yeah, I know," Cade grumbled. "He's *always* right, dammit."

"We can lock this place off," Teclan said. "Fix the com units so they can't be used even if our visitors did get in. Which they won't, once I initiate a security code on the door."

"Let's do it, then," Cade said. "My gut instinct tells me we could be running out of time."

Teclan carried out his securing process, rendering the communications equipment inoperable. He led the way out of the center, then closed the hatch and keyed in a complicated code sequence that locked the heavy door.

"In case of any mishap," Teclan said, "I've given Janek the two sequences, Marshal Cade."

He led the way along to a small airlock, where he tapped in the operating sequence. There was a soft hiss of air being pumped into the lock, followed by the thump of the electro-bolts withdrawing. The airlock door swung open.

Teclan had produced two pairs of magno-boots from a locker.

"Take it easy," Cade said. "I don't want to have to pick you pair up in a paper bag."

"Comforting words, Thomas," Janek said, stamping his feet into the heavy boots.

"Marshal Cade, if you wait outside the weapons center, we'll trip the hatch once we get inside so you can provide cross fire."

"How long will it take us?" Janek asked.

"We could be inside within twenty minutes," Teclan said. "Not counting unforeseen delays, of course."

The cyborgs stepped inside the airlock, and the door swung shut behind them. Cade watched the indicator lights until they showed that the outside airlock door had been opened.

He turned away and started back to the weapons center.

TECLAN MOVED AHEAD, crossing the wide expanse of the satellite's surface with confidence. His intimate knowledge of Skylance's construction and layout allowed him to move about with total freedom.

Janek followed a few yards behind. He was aware how easily his attention might wander if he allowed it.

It was in his nature to want to examine everything. But he felt something more—an overpowering need to check and absorb every detail of his surroundings. This was his first contact with real space. He'd been here before, but always within the confines of a traveling space-craft, surrounded by metal and plastic, protected within the artificial atmosphere that man required to keep him alive. In that environment Janek had been unable to experience total contact with real space. Now he was experiencing that contact and he found it difficult to stay with the reason he was out here.

He forced his mind back to the matter at hand. His appreciation of the vast universe around him would have to wait for another time. Even so, he found the moment deeply satisfying, and retained those feelings within his memory. When he returned to Earth, he planned to discuss them with Dr. Landers at the Cybo Tech facility.

Teclan pointed to the raised outer block of the emergency airlock, then raised a hand, beckoning Janek in close. The airlock stood out from the smooth white surface of the platform, only a few yards from an air-exhaust port.

Together the cyborgs closed in on the airlock, their movement hampered by the cling of the heavy magno-boots to the platform's surface.

They were almost on the airlock when Janek caught a glimpse of something moving. He turned his head and saw the head and shoulders of one of the Amosin combat droids. The droid had its back to them.

Janek touched Teclan's arm and attracted his attention. When Teclan turned, Janek pointed out the combat droid. He indicated that he wanted Teclan to stay put and out of sight.

Cutting off at an angle, Janek moved around the exhaust port, using that as his means of cover. It brought him around on the droid's left side. From his cover Janek could see that the combat droid carried an autorifle. There was also a small walkie-talkie unit clipped to the droid's belt.

Janek judged the distance, taking into account he wasn't going to be able to move quickly. The magnoboots would restrict his ability to hit hard and fast. The only thing to counter that was the fact that the same conditions would slow the combat droid's responses.

Accepting that he couldn't wait too long for a favorable moment, Janek moved the second the droid turned completely away from him, making a visual sweep of the area. Pushing out from behind the exhaust port, Janek struck out for the dark shape of the combat droid. He called up every reserve of strength, pushing hard with his legs, dragging the heavy boots with every step.

The droid turned back in Janek's direction without warning. Janek lunged forward, his arms reaching out. The combat droid registered the cyborg's presence and began to swing the autorifle into position.

Ignoring the risk, Janek launched himself forward, breaking the hold of both magno-boots. He sailed across the intervening gap between himself and the droid, the fingers of his left hand closing around the rifle's barrel and crushing into the steel. He pushed the muzzle away, snatching at the walkie-talkie on the droid's belt. Janek ripped it free and let it drift away. Then his body crashed against the combat droid's, slamming it back against the exhaust port. Janek rammed one foot against the side of the port, regaining a hold on the surface with his magno-boot. Secure, he concentrated on disarming the droid. The droid was resisting violently, pounding at Janek with its free hand, while desperately trying to hang on to the autorifle with the other.

Janek tore the rifle out of the droid's hand, severing two of its fingers in the process. As the weapon floated away, Janek closed the fingers of his left hand around the droid's throat, shoving it back. The combat droid was crushed against the edge of the exhaust port, its metal spine under extreme pressure as Janek kept on pushing, his right hand reaching for the autopistol under his left arm. He ignored the frantic hammering of the droid's fists against his own face and chest. It was only as his pistol slid free and arced into position that Janek relaxed the pressure on the droid's throat. There was a look of triumph on the combat droid's angular face as its head swung back in line with Janek's. The droid imagined its barrage of blows had weakened Janek.

It's triumph was short-lived. As it came face-to-face with Janek, the cyborg shoved the muzzle of his autopistol into the droid's left eye and triggered a rapid trio of soft-nosed slugs that burrowed deep into the droid's metal skull, expanding and destroying its electronic brain. The back of the droid's head split open, spewing a rain of shattered microcircuitry into the vacuum of space.

Janek showed himself to the waiting Teclan, beckoning him over. Teclan walked directly to the airlock. By the time Janek reached him, Teclan had the lock open. As Janek stepped inside, he caught a glimpse of the combat droid, still where he'd left it. The droid, attached to the platform's surface by its magno-boots, swayed gently in time to the platform's orbital movement.

As the outer door swung shut with a solid bump, the electro-clamps locked in place. Teclan keyed in the code, and the lock was flooded with oxygen. As the indicator lights gave the all clear, Teclan glanced across at Janek.

"Okay, you can breathe again now," he joked.

"*I'm* supposed to say things like that to Cade."

"Does he appreciate it?"

"If he's in the right mood," Janek admitted. "If he isn't, he grumbles like hell."

"Humans," Teclan observed.

"They're weird sometimes," Janek said. "But I like them."

Checking their handguns, the cyborgs positioned themselves on either side of the inner lock door. Teclan fingered the access button and the clamps released. The door opened automatically on silent hinges. They emerged into a small, brightly lit chamber where they got out of the magno-boots.

"On the other side of the hatch there," Teclan said, "is the power control room. Directly to the left is the master console. If you can cover me for five seconds, I can shut off the power source. Then all we have to handle are the bad guys themselves."

"Sounds fair," Janek said. Then something occurred to him. "Teclan, is there any kind of warning transmitted to the center telling them the airlock's been used?"

Teclan's head snapped around, his momentary silence indicating to Janek that the answer should have been yes.

"Damn!" Teclan said. "I *forgot*."

"What the hell," Janek said, "we're only human after all!"

He pressed the button to open the hatch leading from the airlock chamber.

As the hatch slid aside, there was a flurry of movement on the other side. An autoweapon opened up, sending a burst of fire through the hatchway. The slugs clanged against the airlock door, flying off the hard steel in all directions. Janek felt one strike his left shoulder. He threw a quick glance at Teclan.

"Give me a chance to clear the place, then follow. You hit that power button. Forget everything else."

Janek ducked low and went through the door, breaking to the right, his back against the bulkhead. He located the source of the firing—a combat droid carrying a military autorifle.

The droid swung in Janek's direction, triggering as it locked on to the cyborg. Janek felt the impact of the bullets against his lower body as the titanium flexi-coat deflected the slugs. He returned fire, angling his pistol up at the droid's skull-like features. The blast of soft-nosed slugs pushed the droid backward. Janek fired a second time, this time his precise aim punching two slugs in through the droid's left eye, destroying its brain and toppling it to the deck where it lay aimlessly thrashing around.

Janek let out a yell. "Teclan!"

The security cyborg charged through the door at Janek's call, leaving the Justice cop to deal with the other occupant of the power control room.

Fleeting seconds had elapsed since Janek had dropped the combat droid. Now the droid's partner, one of Tane's men, rolled from cover, opening up with his own autoweapon. The combat rifle's burst of fire filled the room with its thunderous noise. The weapon was a heavy-caliber model, employing high-impact shells. The mercenary ignored Janek and concentrated his firepower on Teclan, realizing where the security cyborg was heading. The sheer impact of the slugs against Teclan's back hurled him across the room. He crashed up against the console, his left arm slipping limply to his side.

Janek yanked his pistol around and locked on to his target. He triggered a burst into the man's exposed body, seeing him twist over on his back while a ragged moan burst from his lips. The gunman's chest was a raw bleeding mess where Janek's bullets had ripped into him. Janek fired a second time, driving a single slug into the skull.

Janek reached Teclan's side just in time to see the cybo depress the switch that cut the power to the weapons center.

"You okay?" Janek asked.

Teclan nodded. "Couple of those slugs cut the function modes to my left arm," he said. "If they can't fix it, I'll have to go on welfare."

Janek grinned. "You can go on TV with a sense of humor like that."

"First let's clear the rats from my station," Teclan said.

The hatch slid open at Teclan's touch, and the pair of cyborgs went through, breaking left and right. An eruption of gunfire filled the vast control room.

Janek cut across the center, making for the console housing the secondary keypad that activated the main hatch. He confronted the guard stationed there and backhanded him with a blow that spun him across the floor. After he keyed in the number sequence that freed the main hatch, Janek turned back to the firefight that was about to determine final control of Skylance.

CADE SAW the hatch begin to open. He could hear the crackle of gunfire from inside the weapons center. The second the hatch widened enough to allow him through, he went in, his autopistol searching for a target.

He caught a glimpse of a moving figure clad in a white pressure suit. One of Tane's men. He was half running, half crawling across the smooth white deck of the weapons center. A heavy spattering of blood stained the front of his suit, and his face was streaked as more blood gushed from a badly crushed nose. Somewhere along the line he seemed to have lost his weapon.

As Cade eased through the hatch, he realized the mercenary was heading directly for him. The man hadn't seen Cade. He seemed to be more interested in getting out of the center. At the last moment he spotted Cade and tried to avoid contact. He twisted his body to one side, but couldn't get out of the way of the looping forearm smash that lashed across his throat. His feet lost contact with the deck, and he curved up and back, crashing heavily to the deck. The back of his skull hit with a hard crack, and blood sprayed out from under it.

Gunfire blasted its way, into Cade's consciousness, and he saw sparks fly from a cabinet close by. The Justice cop lunged forward, swinging his handgun around to track in on the gunman, and he saw one of the Amosin combat droids level its weapon for a second shot. Cade returned fire on the move, triggering his pistol at the droid's head. He saw the droid jerk back, the slugs burning dark streaks across its face. Then he was down on one knee, steadying the muzzle of the autopistol on the droid as it recovered and turned back to engage him again. Dismissing the risk to himself, Cade held off from firing until he had the droid dead to rights. He triggered, once, twice, hammering a pair of .357 Magnums through the droid's right eye and terminating the combat droid.

Something smashed down between Cade's shoulders, slamming the breath from his lungs. He sprawled facedown across the deck, rolling quickly, and saw another droid standing over him. The droid held an autorifle. The weapon must have been out of ammunition, and instead of firing, the droid had swung it like a club. Cade sensed the heavy butt lashing at his face and tried to roll clear. It caught him across the back of his right shoulder, numbing him. Cade kicked out, and his booted foot slammed against the droid's knee. The impact knocked the droid briefly off balance as its foot slipped on the smooth deck. The respite was short, but enough to give Cade the chance to scramble clear and gain his feet. He yanked the reserve gun from his belt and jammed it into the droid's face as it lunged back toward him. He triggered a sustained blast that drilled into the droid's skull and blew it apart.

Across the weapons center, Cade caught a blurred glimpse of Janek trading shots with another of the Amosin droids.

He heard a single shot and felt a burning sensation across his ribs on the right side. Glancing down, he saw dark blood soaking through his clothing and realized he'd been hit.

He shook himself the way a dog does to shake water off its hide and swung around to pick up on the shooter.

He saw a wild-eyed mercenary, still clutching the weapon he'd used, turning his head as a cyborg clad in a white jumpsuit closed in on him. Teclan slapped the merc's gun aside, grabbing the man with his good arm and swinging him up over his head. The man screamed once before Teclan hurled him bodily across the center. The twisting body was smashed against the far bulkhead with enough force to shatter the skull. The dead man slithered down the curve of the bulkhead to roll into a bloody, crumpled heap on the deck.

"T.J., down!" Janek's voice bellowed.

Cade didn't ask why. He simply dropped, hitting the deck hard, the autopistol bouncing from his hand and skidding across the floor. He caught a glimpse of a shadow close behind him.

The harsh rattle of an autoweapon drowned all other sound. Something brushed Cade's foot. He twisted his head and saw the heavy shape of a combat droid's boot. The droid was returning fire. Hot shell casings fell like snowflakes around Cade.

Glancing across the center, Cade saw Janek. The cyborg stood his ground as he traded shots with the combat droid. Cade saw a couple of slugs strike Janek's upper body, making him reel backward.

Cade shoved himself to his feet and lurched at the combat droid. He rammed his shoulder into the droid's side, pushing it briefly off balance. The droid made an angry sound and swung one big, powerful hand in Cade's direction. The blow caught the Justice cop across the side of the face, sending him spinning across the deck.

The distraction gave Janek the opportunity he needed. Angling the muzzle of his weapon, the cyborg emptied the rest of the magazine into the droid's skull. The droid swung around, emitting a harsh screech of sound. Its fingers jammed down hard on the trigger of its rifle. The half-full magazine was blasted at almost point-blank range against the bulkhead. The high-velocity slugs struck at a point where there were no heavy pieces of equipment to slow their passage.

A high crack of sound was immediately followed by the shrill warning sirens. Warning lights began to flash, and the open hatch started to close, sealing off the weapons center.

With a whoosh air began to rush out through the punctured bulkhead, and pressure dropped with alarming speed. The damaged area expanded from a few ragged holes to a six-inch rent in the bulkhead as the weapons center depressurized. Loose objects were dragged through the air, crashing against the bulkhead, all being dragged in the direction of the rupture.

"Janek," Teclan yelled. "For Cade."

The security cyborg thrust an emergency oxygen cylinder and mask into Janek's hand, then turned to grab something from a locker.

Janek, fighting against the relentless drag of the lowering pressure, struggled in Cade's direction.

The weapons center was filled by a howling noise, and the rush of air was lowering the temperature.

Cade, already starting to feel weak from the loss of air, had wedged himself into a gap between two of the electronic units. He could feel the drag of the escaping pressure. It threatened to haul him from his safe hole and splatter him across the bulkhead. His lungs were beginning to burn from being denied oxygen, and despite trying to keep control, he could feel the spidery fingers of panic breaking down his resolve.

The problem was he didn't know where to go, and even if he did, he couldn't risk moving.

He thought the lights were dimming, then realized he was starting to pass out.

He wanted to yell, to scream his defiance. This was no way to die, trapped in some metal coffin floating above the Earth. But he couldn't even voice his feelings. There was no strength left in him. It was all draining away—just like the air screaming out through the tear in the bulkhead.

Hands grabbed him, yanked him into a sitting position. Cade stared up through blurred eyes. He saw a hazy face topped by white-blond hair. Then a rubbery mask was jammed across his mouth and he began to breathe in the purest, sweetest air he'd ever tasted. He gulped it down, choking and gasping until he got control.

"Don't know how you ever manage without me," Janek intoned, his face deadpan.

Cade didn't say a word. For once he was speechless. Getting air back into his starved lungs was more important than getting the better of Janek.

Over his partner's shoulder Cade watched Teclan place a square pad of thick, flexible material over the rupture in the bulkhead. The magnetic square sealed the gap and would hold long enough for Teclan to assign the service droids to make a permanent repair. With the pressure eased, Janek was able to get Cade back on his feet. Along with Teclan, they quit the weapons center. Teclan punched the button to close and seal the hatch.

Cade's final view of the center showed a mercenary lying in a crumpled, bloody heap. The man had been dragged across the deck by the force of the pressure drop and jammed against the side of a computer console, his dead face crushed out of shape as the drag of the escaping air had tried to pull him through a too-small gap.

The massive hatch closed with a final thud.

Cade slipped the oxygen mask from his face. He breathed in the clean, filtered air from Skylance's purifiers.

"No offence, Teclan," he said, "but I can't wait to get off this platform and back to Earth."

"You don't like it up here?" Teclan asked. "I know it's been rough. . . ."

Janek shook his head. "It isn't that," he said. "We've a case to close back home. And it won't wait."

14

Janek docked the shuttle, cutting the power. As the whine of the motors faded, he saw a refueling tender approaching, followed by an open truck carrying a team of maintenance droids. Quitting the pilot's seat, the cyborg crossed to where Cade was standing by the hatch. Janek watched his partner make a final check of the autopistol before jamming it back in its holster and closing his jacket.

"This is where it could get touchy, T.J.," Janek said. "How do we play it?"

"Official, if we can. Make up the rules if it turns hot," Cade replied with conviction.

"Sounds good to me."

"Let's do it without too much chatter, Janek," Cade said as the hatch began to open. "I hurt all over. My ribs ache where that bullet bounced off. I'm feeling pretty beat-up, so don't be smart. Okay?"

Janek shrugged awkwardly, clicking his teeth in frustration. The more he tried to pull a shrug off correctly, the more he looked deformed.

"You're no fun anymore, Marshal Cade," Janek said accusingly. "I should have stayed on Skylance with Teclan. Hey, I bet he treats Curtis better than you're treating me."

"Prisoners have rights," Cade said pointedly.

Without waiting for a reply, he walked down the ramp as it slid out to lock on the base of the hatch. Cade crossed the docking bay, flashing his Justice badge at the security droid on duty. The droid took its time scanning the bar code. Janek watched it from a distance, seeing the droid edge its right hand close to the butt of the handgun holstered in its belt. He swung around the back of the droid and came up close, jamming the muzzle of his own weapon against the droid's eye.

"You wouldn't want to be found obstructing Justice Department business, would you?" the cyborg suggested quietly.

The security droid hesitated. "My orders were to look out for Marshals Cade and Janek."

"Orders from who?" Cade asked, relieving the droid of its weapon.

"Police Chief Norris."

"Since when did Norris have jurisdiction over Newark?" Janek asked. "He's only chief in New York."

"I only work for Security Systems," the droid explained. "Our head office is in New York."

Cade peered at the droid's ID tag. "You've got a choice, 663. Call this in and break the law, or cooperate with us."

The droid turned and scanned Janek, aware he was dealing with an advanced cyborg.

"What would you do?" it asked. "I'm programmed to serve and protect. I'm supposed to stay within the law, but I'm obligated to do as my supervisor tells me." The droid made a vague gesture. "This isn't going to be my day."

"Turn us in," Janek said, "and you assist in a conspiracy against the legal government."

The droid sighed. Then it brightened.

"I have a thought. If I'm deactivated, I can't do *anything*. Can I?"

The droid led Janek across to a storage locker and opened the door. It stepped inside, turning its back to the CB. Janek opened the droid's jacket and exposed the small access panel in its side. He opened it and keyed in the sequence that cut the droid's power supply. The security droid instantly shut off. Janek closed the door and locked it.

"Let's get out of here," Janek said.

They cut across the docking bay, heading in the direction of the service hangars. Threading their way through the busy maintenance bays, they emerged on the far side and walked through the administration offices.

"Hey, who let you guys in here?"

Cade faced the heavyset man who stepped out of an office. He was dressed in crumpled clothes, and his unshaven face was pockmarked.

"Justice Department," Cade said, showing his badge.

The man studied it, squinting his small, hostile eyes. "Maybe you got that out of a packet of cereal," he said, smirking at his own humor.

"Same one you got your IQ, maybe," Janek snapped.

The man spun around on the cybo. "Smartass. Maybe you want I should toss you outta here."

"Go ahead," Janek said. "Make the best of it 'cause you'll have plenty of time dreaming about it in the lockup."

The man shrugged. "So what do you want?"

"How about some privacy?" Cade suggested. "And a phone?"

The man relented, seeing no point in hassling a couple of Justice cops. He knew they could carry through any of the threats they might make. The last thing he needed was trouble with the cops. His old lady was enough for him to handle.

"In there," he said, pointing to an empty dispatch office.

"Thank you for your cooperation," Janek said as the man slouched off. Then the cyborg stationed himself at the door while Cade picked up the phone and punched in a number.

Milt Schuberg's face swam into focus on the vidscreen. "Jesus, am I glad to see you, Cade. How'd it go?"

"It went," Cade said. "You all set?"

Schuberg nodded. "We got all kinds of shit going down. Something is definitely happening. Whole department's being reassigned. New people being moved into key positions. Ask questions and all you get is told to butt out and do your job."

"Time to move, Milt. Watch your back...this could get bloody."

"Yeah? Well, I feel pretty bloody myself," Schuberg announced. "I don't like what's goin' on, and there are going to be some asses kicked."

"Be in touch, Milt."

"Where you heading?"

"I've a message to deliver to Sinclair. In person."

Cade put down the phone and rejoined Janek. "Milt's on it," he said. "Now let's go find ourselves a ride upstate."

Out in the dispatch yard Cade looked around for a suitable vehicle. He spotted an air cruiser belonging to a courier service. The driver had gone off to hand in his packages to the delivery office, leaving the cruiser unattended. Cade crossed to the cruiser and accessed the hatch. Janek followed. As Cade fired up the turbo-boosted General Motors power plant, the hatch locked with hiss of hydraulics. Keying in the hover mode, Cade took the cruiser up and out of the dispatch yard. Once he'd achieved the height he wanted, he changed to forward power and the cruiser headed across country.

Cade nodded to his partner. "See if you can get through to Braddock. Tell him what we've got. He'll need to push it through to Washington so the department can get a line on the conspirators there."

Janek picked up the cruiser's handset and keyed in a transmission code on the phone. The code was for Braddock's personal phone line. The call was answered instantly, and Braddock's face filled the cruiser's vid-screen.

"Where the hell have you guys been?" Braddock asked.

"You don't want to know," Janek said. "Braddock, we've got to move fast. Got some names for you. They need to be removed from action. And watch your back...there's a lot of queer stuff going on."

Janek reeled off names and laid out the details of the conspiracy as briefly as he could. The cyborg didn't want to stay on the line any longer than necessary, in case there was a tap on the department phones. Braddock had thoughts along similar lines, so he didn't question Janek's information. He simply accepted it and cut the connection. Janek ended the session and leaned back in his seat.

"Are you in control of this damn thing?" he asked as Cade cut around the rear of a slow-moving air freighter and dodged a floating advertising drone.

"Got my license years ago."

"I wasn't asking that," the cyborg said tersely.

"You don't trust me?"

"On the ground, okay," Janek said. "Up here I like to feel I'm in good hands."

Cade increased the power, taking the cruiser to its maximum altitude as he approached Manhattan. He skirted the edge of the city, turning the cruiser to the north, and followed the gleaming ribbon of the Hudson as he moved upstate.

"What if Sinclair isn't home?" Janek asked.

"I'm banking on him staying put. Amosin will be his command base. He'll be worried because Skylance hasn't been in contact for a while. But he isn't about to quit now—he's in so deep. Until he has to accept his scheme's gone sour, he'll hang on. This is his last chance, Janek, and he won't let go easily."

"I bow to your superior intellect," the cyborg intoned mirthlessly.

The cruiser's speaker system began to crackle. Jumbled sounds filled the compartment, then a voice broke through as a trace locked onto the cruiser's waveband.

"Cruiser S422-NYS. This is the NYPD air-traffic authority. You are in violation of city regulations. Request you land at emergency pad 67 immediately."

Cade snatched up the phone and keyed the transmit button.

"Listen up, air traffic. This is T. J. Cade, Justice marshal. Don't interfere with department business. I don't give a damn who issued your orders, and I suggest you go back to chasing speedsters. Leave me alone or I'll land this damn thing on your roof and come down to kick your butts."

"Tough talk, Cade, but we got instructions from Chief Norris to nail your ass...."

"Norris is through," Cade snapped back. "I'm yanking his badge before today's over, so figure out who goes down with him if you follow his orders. Your choice, boys."

He cut the connection, swearing under his breath as he took the cruiser in a long power drive over the river.

Janek clamped his lips shut tight, deciding now was not a good time to ask if he could take a vacation. Instead, the cyborg searched his circuits for a jazz station. He locked on to a concert by a visiting Chicago combo, and silently lost himself in the music, while he continued to monitor the sky around them.

Suddenly he became alert. "Hey, watch out," he said, but the next second he was thrown to one side as the air cruiser lurched violently. As the cyborg righted himself, he caught a glimpse of a dark shape looming alongside.

It was a matt black combat helicopter. The pilot was using the chopper's rotor wash to push the lighter air cruiser off course.

Janek started to say something, but his words were lost as Cade pushed the cruiser into a steep dive, taking it away from the menacing helicopter. The cruiser, built for more sedate travel, groaned and creaked as pressure built up along its seams.

Twisting around in his seat, Janek located the chopper. It was curving down in their wake, lining up for a clear shot from its nose-mounted rotary cannon.

"Get us the hell out of here," Janek said. "I think you annoyed that pilot to no end."

"*He's* annoyed! I'm not in that good a mood myself."

Light winked from the barrels of the rotary cannon. A stream of shells cut the air around the cruiser, some scoring the hull.

Cade yanked the controls, almost turning the cruiser over as he executed a series of maneuvers the designers hadn't even dreamed of for the craft. As he pushed it into an extreme turn, something cracked with a sharp sound, and the controls became sluggish.

"See," Janek reprimanded. "See. I told you."

"Hang on," Cade yelled above the noise.

The cruiser sank like a stone, and the ground rushed up to meet them. A stretch of forested countryside lay below. Cade didn't pull up until the last moment, allowing the air cruiser to crash its way through the uppermost branches of the trees. The thin alloy of the cruiser was ripped open. A trail of debris trailed behind the craft.

Spotting a clearing ahead, Cade angled the cruiser toward it, taking a reckless chance at landing. The cruiser struck the soft ground bouncing wildly. Cade hit the retro jets, feeling the cruiser shudder and yaw to the right. Losing its flight capability, the aircraft became a dead weight. It careered violently, slithering in a wide arc, and came to an abrupt stop against a tree. The canopy shattered, showering Cade and Janek with Plexiglas as they were thrown forward against the seat restraints.

Janek twisted around as he picked up the noise of the combat chopper. A shadow began to slide across the ground, converging on the downed cruiser.

"Time to move on," he said, thumping the emergency-hatch release.

They cleared the cruiser seconds before a raking blast from the chopper's cannon tore through the passenger compartment. The heat blast from the cruiser's exploding fuel tank singed their clothing as they hit the ground, scrambling for safety. Flaming fuel rained down around them, fanned by the rotor wash from the settling chopper.

Cade pulled his autopistol, peering through the swirl of smoke from the burning cruiser. He watched the three-man team jump from the helicopter, their combat rifles at the ready as they began to spread, fanning out to pick up any trail.

Before the strike team had moved more than a few yards, Cade loomed out of the smoke, his autopistol crackling as he laid down a deadly burst.

The closest mercenary caught a trio of .357 slugs in his throat that slapped him to the ground. Turning the moment he'd fired, Cade took out the second one, laying two shots into his chest and a third in the back of his skull as he was spun around.

The surviving mercenary swung his rifle on Cade, his finger already pressuring the trigger when something solid struck him between the shoulders. He was thrown to the ground, and his rifle bounced from his hands. Pain spread through him like a wild burn, coring deep into his chest cavity, then leaving him numb.

Cade picked up one of the rifles and made for the idling chopper. Behind him Janek jammed his still-smoking pistol back in its holster, selected a weapon for himself and followed.

"Let's go," Cade snapped as Janek slid into the pilot's seat.

"Can I strap in first? Time you took some stress counseling, Thomas. Times are when you're a real pain."

"Just stress this damn thing off the ground, Janek."

The cyborg powered the chopper's motors. It rose quickly, and Janek set the course that would bring them over Amos Sinclair's sprawling estate.

"Should get us there in a little under two minutes," Janek said.

Cade swung his seat around and checked the chopper's rear compartment. An array of weapons was clipped to a rack against the bulkhead, including SMGs and assault rifles. There were also throwaway rocket launchers with armor-piercing missiles.

"Janek, it's like Christmas in July back here."

"You want to translate that for me, T.J.?"

Cade picked out one of the rocket launchers and waved it under Janek's nose.

"So Sinclair wants to start a revolution? I'll show that son of a bitch how to stop one. The hard way."

Janek groaned. "I just knew you were going to say that."

Ahead of them they picked out the fenced-off estate.

An indicator light began to flash. Moments later a voice came through the speaker system, asking for the chopper's ID code.

"Well, don't look at me," Janek protested. "Just figure us a way out."

"Sinclair doesn't miss a trick," Cade said.

"Neither will they," Janek said meaningfully, and Cade followed his gaze.

A pair of choppers identical to their own were rising from the grounds of the Sinclair estate, locking on to a course that would bring them on line for an attack.

"No pain, no gain," Cade said through gritted teeth, and reached for the rotary cannon's control system. He swung the handset into position and slipped on the helmet that would lock him into the weapons system. The laser-enhanced fire control, relayed through the helmet, enabled the wearer to lock on to the target through a high-definition display. The rotary cannon would track the target by following the wearer's eye movement.

Activating the weapons system, Cade picked up the first of the ascending combat choppers. He keyed in range information and directed the on-board computer to provide coordinates. As they flashed up on the helmet display, Cade locked in on the chopper, waited the requested time span to bring the target within effective range, then opened fire.

The 30 mm rotary cannon, set in the nose of the chopper, exploded with sound. Its six barrels sent a stream of armor-piercing shells at the distant chopper. They caught the chopper's whirling rotors and blew them apart, then dropped to chew ragged holes in the fuselage. The chopper began to fall away, spinning out of control.

Janek angled his machine away from the second chopper, which was still climbing and at a disadvantage. The cyborg used their height and speed to bring him in on the other chopper's tail, giving Cade the opportunity to gain target acquisition and repeat his performance with the cannon. The blast of fire tore through the chopper's fuselage, puncturing the fuel tanks and turning the crippled machine into a ball of expanding flame.

"Okay, hotshot," Cade said, "let's get down there before they send anything else at us."

Janek put the chopper in a long dive that took them inside the estate's boundary fences. He flew across the wide expanses of expertly tended lawns and gardens, heading the chopper toward Sinclair's massive residence. On a wide concrete pad were a number of combat choppers, two of them with spinning rotors.

"In close," Cade directed.

He targeted the chopper pad and raked the standing machines with cannon fire, reducing the sophisticated military hardware to burning hulks and their crews to shriveled corpses. As Janek overflew the pad, he saw armed figures running for cover.

Dumping the helmet, Cade swiveled his seat. He began to arm himself with weaponry, aware that there was going to be fierce resistance the moment Janek put the chopper down. His choices, in addition to an assault rifle with spare magazines, were rocket launchers and a loop of stun grenades.

As the combat helicopter touched down, Janek cut the power. He also armed himself from the rack, adding a number of the rocket launchers to his selection along with a belt holding HE grenades.

Cade had already unsealed the hatch and was out of the chopper. Janek landed on the far side of the concrete pad, using the drifting smoke from the burning helicopters to provide temporary cover.

"Every man and cyborg for himself," Cade said as Janek joined him, but Janek merely punched him in the arm, not deigning to say anything in reply.

They pushed through the smoke and emerged on the far side, with the wrecked choppers between them and the house.

"Vehicle coming," Janek warned. "On your left."

Cade picked up the roar of the motor. He hefted one of the rocket launchers and unclipped the safety cover, automatically priming the launcher.

As the 4x4 emerged from the smoke, Cade dropped to one knee, the launcher over his shoulder, his eye pressed to the inbuilt laser sight. He settled the red dot on the 4x4's front and depressed the button. The launcher coughed, and a jet of flame gushed from the end of the tube as the missile fired. It sped toward the truck, locked on target. The explosion flipped the shattered vehicle over on its back, and it skidded across the ground, spilling its six-man crew in all directions.

Janek, moving in from the flank, picked off the three men who managed to survive. His assault rifle put them down for good, the stream of slugs tearing them apart before they had a chance to use their own weapons.

With Cade in the lead, they made an all-out dash for the house. The layout was familiar to them from their previous visit, saving them valuable seconds as they broke through to the patio area.

Resistance heated up then, and the rattle of small-arms fire greeted them as they skirted the area. Taking cover behind the low wall, Cade and Janek reviewed the situation.

"We've got eight, maybe nine guns between us and the house," Janek said. "And there could be more ready to back them."

Cade unlimbered his second launcher and activated it.

"You ready to go over the wall when this explodes?"

"The tradition is to toss a coin to see who goes," Janek grumbled.

"You wouldn't want to admit to using old-fashioned methods like that."

"If it saves my ass—yes!"

Cade grinned. He laid the launcher across the top of the wall and fired. The missile struck on the far side of the pool, sending a shower of patio tiles into the air. Water began to fountain up from a ruptured pipe.

Janek rolled over the wall when the answering fire petered out for a second. He was on his feet and running before they opened up again.

A pair of uniformed men broke cover as they spotted the cyborg, their weapons turning in Janek's direction.

He kept on moving forward, the assault rifle tracking in on its targets. Janek triggered the weapon and blew them both off their feet in sprays of misty red. He half turned as he caught hurried movement off to his right, then traded shots with another attacker. That one went down with ragged holes in both legs, clutching at his shattered limbs.

Reaching the cover of the side of the house, Janek paused to scan the area. He picked up one gunman firing across the pool. Janek saw Cade cutting across the far side of the patio, weaving as he tried to avoid the deadly stream of the merc's slugs. Janek shouldered his assault rifle and snap-aimed. He triggered a single shot and saw the merc's head jerk sideways as a gout of dark fluid erupted from his skull.

Cade had completed his run for the far side of the pool, crossing the patio in an uninterrupted dash. As he approached the wide picture window that led inside the house, he lifted the rifle and triggered a burst. The bullets bounced off the shatterproof glass. Cade unhitched his last rocket launcher, primed it and fired. The missile hit the glass and exploded, blowing the great expanse of glass into the house.

Tossing aside the empty tube, Cade brought his rifle into action as he stormed the house, firing in through the now-open window. He caught sight of movement on the far side of the smoke-filled room, spotting the gleam of metal as someone turned an autoweapon on him. Cade took a sideways dive, landed on his shoulder and rolled. He could hear and feel the march of bullets tearing into the thick carpeting in his wake. He came to a stop against a holo-vid player and pulled himself into cover.

He heard a man yelling defiantly, still firing blind. Hot lead tore into floor and walls, gouging and chewing away at the expensive decor.

Cade rolled to the far end of the wide holo-vid unit and pushed to his feet. He located the figure of the man doing all the shooting.

The uniform gave him away. It was Colonel Clayton Munro. He was facing Cade now, anger clouding his features.

"Goddamn it, Cade, you had to keep pushing! Couldn't leave it alone. We almost had it made. Another few hours, and we'd have had it all."

"It's over now, Munro," Cade called. "Give it up. Your way wasn't the right one."

"It had to be done!" Munro yelled.

"Throw down the gun, Munro. Now!"

Clayton Munro ignored the request. He moved, swinging across the room so he could expose Cade.

Cade saw his strategy. He didn't hesitate. The assault rifle came on line, catching Munro's figure as he stepped into view. Cade pulled the trigger. The impact slammed the colonel against the wall, spattering it with bright beads of blood. Munro gave a low groan, rolling around to face the wall. His fingers splayed out, slithering across the smooth surface as the renegade colonel lost his struggle with life and went down.

Cade gained his feet and crossed the room in long strides. A wide archway led him through to an even larger, luxuriously appointed room. One wall was composed of high-tech audio and visual equipment. On the far side of the room, wide double doors opened on a spacious walkway that pushed deeper into the vast house.

Cade reached the doors, peering around the edge of the wall.

An autopistol fired, and a long splinter of wood was torn from the door frame. As he jerked his head back under cover, Cade spotted a group of people making their way along the wide walkway.

He made out the uniformed figure of Colonel Edwin Poole. Just ahead of Poole was Amos Sinclair. There was a trio of civilians dressed in expensive suits, and Chief of Police Norris in his NYPD dress uniform. They were all in a ring of armed mercenaries, backed up by Lukas Tane himself. The group was moving purposefully, headed deeper into Sinclair's expansive home.

Cade saw it as running.

The conspirators had accepted their plan wasn't going as well as it should. Now they were looking for a way out, an escape from the results of their crimes.

"No damn way!" Cade muttered to himself, jamming a fresh mag into the assault rifle. He slammed the bolt back, cocking the weapon, and broke cover.

The gunman who had fired the warning shot saw the Justice cop erupt from the doorway and swung up his autopistol for what he figured would be an easy shot.

Cade got there first, his actions generated by a burning need to stop Sinclair and his followers.

The assault rifle slammed out its sound, and a trio of bullets caught the merc in the chest, driving him to the floor.

The other gunmen closed ranks around their charges, moving them at a faster rate.

Cade, keeping his back to a wall, stalked them, waiting for his chance.

He saw one pause to lift his weapon. Cade's shot took him in the left shoulder and knocked him off balance, making him fall against one of his own. The action caused a ripple of unease to run through the protected group. A man began to protest until Lukas Tane shouted him down.

Cade used the moment of panic to lay down a burst of rapid fire that cut into the line of armed men, dropping two of them and wounding another.

The group broke apart as Tane's mercenaries laid down a covering round of loose fire. They were attempting to protect the unarmed section at the same time, so their fire was erratic.

Breaking a stun grenade from the loop he carried on his belt, Cade flicked off the breakaway cap, priming the egg-shaped device. He tossed it, then turned his head away and covered his ears. He heard the grenade detonate, the sound muffled to his protected ears. As the echo died away, Cade turned back. A thick cloud of smoke filled the walkway, and he could hear groaning. When the smoke began to clear, Cade saw a number of figures down on their hands and knees, blood trickling from noses and ears.

The assault rifle tracking ahead of him, Cade advanced on the scattered group. He triggered the weapon hard and fast, taking out the mercs who were already reaching for their weapons, though still dazed.

The next moment, Janek joined him, and added his firepower to his partner's. Between them they drove the remnants of Lukas Tane's mercenary group to the floor.

The last line defense of the mercenaries allowed the remainder of the straggling, desperate group, including Sinclair and Edwin Poole, to reach the far end of the walkway. A sliding door opened to allow them through. The last man to leave was Lukas Tane himself.

Cade caught a glimpse of daylight on the opposite side of the door. "Move it, Janek," he yelled. "They'll have transport out there somewhere."

He put on a burst of speed that brought him to the door in a rush. Cade was ready to burst through in pursuit. Before he did, Janek shouldered him to one side. As Cade stumbled, banging against the inside wall, he heard a heavy concentration of autofire, and out of the corner of his eye he saw Janek reel back as he took a number of hits in his midsection.

Cade glanced through the door.

Striding toward it, weapons up and firing, were three of the Amosin combat droids. The black-clad figures were directing their combined fire at Janek.

One swung up a heavy, squat piece of hardware that Cade recognized as a grenade launcher. The droid leveled the weapon and touched the trigger, sending a small, powerful minigrenade winging toward Janek.

The cyborg twisted his body violently, managing to avoid the grenade's full blast. But there was enough impact in the explosion to spin Janek off his feet, his left leg disintegrating in a blur of flying fragments.

Janek felt his leg give way. He reached up and snatched the remaining launcher swinging from his shoulder, fingers activating the firing system even as he fell. He thrust out one hand, bracing himself as he struck the floor. Pulling the tube around, he leveled it at the bunched combat droids and fired. The launcher gushed flame as the missile burst from the tube. It struck the center droid and detonated with a blinding flash. The trio was engulfed in the explosion that followed, the impact ripping them apart and spewing debris into the air.

"Go!" Janek said. "I'm fine, so don't stand there staring."

Cade ducked through the door, stepping over the smoking remains of the combat droids.

He was faced by a wide, curving concourse that provided access to Amosin's production facility. A gleaming monorail swept across the concrete apron, offering comfortable transportation to anyone needing to travel deep into the production complex. To the left was a fully equipped helipad, with four machines parked on it. Two bore military markings. A third belonged to the NYPD.

Cade oriented himself with a sweeping glance as he located his targets.

Colonel Edwin Poole had stopped running. He was facing Cade, sunlight glancing off the gleaming medals pinned to his uniform. He was in the act of pulling his service automatic from his uniform tunic, an expression of utter resignation on his face.

Across from Poole, the NYPD chief, Norris, was hurriedly squeezing his uniformed bulk into the hatch of his helicopter. Norris threw a hasty glance over his shoulder, sensing Cade's approach. Confirmation of his suspicions forced him to move too quickly. He missed his footing and slipped from the hatch, slithering down the shiny curve of the chopper's gleaming black fuselage. The renegade cop stumbled awkwardly, broad face red and sweaty, remaining bent over for a few seconds. When he began to straighten, he had a gun in his hand.

The three civilians, now recognizable as local politicians and one state senator, had thrown themselves to the ground at the sound of combat.

Amos Sinclair, shielded by Lukas Tane, was cutting across the concourse. The industrialist was leading his bodyguard toward the monorail access platform.

Cade assessed the situation in one swift take, marking his prime targets and acting on that information.

He swung up the assault rifle and locked on to the bulky torso of Chief Norris. The cop already had his weapon out and leveled, finger squeezing back on the trigger.

The boom of Cade's weapon drowned out the sharp cry of pain that burst from Norris's lips. Cade's slug caught him in the upper chest, slamming him back against the side of the chopper. Feebly he lifted his weapon to return fire. Cade's next bullet caught him in the neck, and a gout of blood arced from the wound. Norris fell over backward, turning in mid-fall, his arms thrown wide. He crashed against the fuselage of the chopper, sliding down it with a curious limpness and flopping facedown on the concourse.

The muzzle of Cade's weapon flicked across to pinpoint Edwin Poole. The black muzzle of Poole's military-issue handgun had locked on target when the sound of a third shot split the air. He was hit between the eyes, and the handgun flipped from his suddenly nerveless fingers and clattered on the concrete. Moments later Poole lay sprawled across the concrete, the back of his shattered skull leaking blood.

Cade glanced behind him and saw Janek, propped against the wall, his smoking assault rifle in his hands.

"Thanks," Cade said.

"Go get Sinclair," Janek said. "I can tie things up here."

Cade worked his way past the helicopters, using them as cover. Peering across the concourse, he saw that Sinclair and Tane had made it into one of the sleek monorail cars. It was already picking up speed as it followed the steel rail that would take it into the complex.

Cade broke cover and ran for the access platform. He pulled open the hatch of the waiting car and settled in the padded seat. He scanned the control panel and was pleased to see that the operation of the cars had been simplified in the extreme. Cade keyed in the start sequence and felt the car glide forward. He punched in maximum speed. The bullet-shaped vehicle burned its way along the shiny steel rail.

Shortly the concourse snaked its way into the complex. Buildings rose on either side in a blur as the car hurtled by. Cade could see the other car in the far distance.

He felt the car begin to slow, then saw that the monorail was descending. It dropped below ground level. As daylight faded, it was replaced by brilliant strip lights embedded in the sides and roof of the curving tunnel the car was in. An interior light came on inside the car.

Cade took the time to reload the assault rifle and his handgun. He got rid of the other gear he'd been carrying.

A light began to flash on the control panel. On a small screen a readout told him the car was slowing due to a blockage on the rail ahead. Cade sat impatiently as the car slowed to a walk, then stopped altogether. He could see the blockage now. It was the car Sinclair and

Tane had been· in. The industrialist had stopped it in order to block the rail. As his car stopped, Cade leaned forward, examining the interior of the stalled car ahead. It was empty and the hatch was open.

"Son of a gun," Cade exclaimed.

The Plexiglas canopy of his car exploded as a furious burst of fire tore through it. Cade dropped to the floor of the car, cursing his own stupidity. Lukas Tane would be laughing his head off! He had set a simple trap, and Cade had stepped right into it.

More shots. This time they were aimed lower down, at the body of the car. Cade winced as the bullets tore through the metal skin and over his prone body. He couldn't stay here for much longer. Tane would move in soon.

Reaching out, Cade unlocked the hatch on the far side of the car. Then he wriggled around and kicked the hatch open. It swung wide and clanked against the body. Cade took a deep breath and rolled across the floor of the car and out the open hatch. He fell clear and crashed down to the concrete below the monorail support column. The impact on landing drove the breath from his body, but Cade was aware he couldn't lie there for too long.

He snatched up the assault rifle, dragging his legs under him, and crawled along the concrete until he'd put a good few yards between the car and himself. Then he flattened himself against the side of the tunnel, trying to keep his harsh breathing down to a soft hiss.

Lukas Tane was around somewhere, maybe even closer than Cade suspected. The mercenary would be in a killing mood now, more so than at any time previously. Not only had Cade and Janek blown the conspiracy all to hell, but they had also decimated Tane's mercenary force. The elimination of Tane's group was certain to reduce the man's credibility to zero—and credibility was the lifeblood of a mercenary soldier's existence. If he couldn't be trusted to carry out an assignment, there weren't going to be any more jobs. That would hurt Tane's pride more than his bank balance.

Cade picked up a shadow of movement. It came from the upper level of the tunnel. He glanced along the curve of the tunnel and saw the concrete steps leading up from the base. He hurried to the steps and went up. There was a walkway extending along the tunnel, just above the steel rail itself. On silent feet Cade moved along the walkway, going in the direction that would lead him farther into the complex.

He neared the curve in the tunnel where he'd spotted the movement.

A shot gouged the concrete above his head, dusting him with powder. Cade dropped to his knees, pushing the rifle ahead of him, eyes searching the walkway. He caught a glimpse of light bouncing off the end of a gun barrel barely showing from behind a support pillar. Cade shouldered his rifle, using the laser sight to pinpoint his target. He stroked the trigger, and the rifle recoiled against his shoulder, the shot echoing along the tunnel. Cade was rewarded by the sight of the extended rifle barrel jerking sharply to the side. A moment later he heard it clatter to the concrete. Using the opportunity, Cade broke cover and sprinted along the walkway. He wanted to reach Tane before the man could rearm himself.

As he closed in on the pillar concealing Tane, Cade saw movement. A dark figure swung out from behind the pillar, and light flashed on the blade of a knife. Cade drew back as Tane slashed at him, the blade slicing through his clothing and leaving a burning line across his chest. The Justice cop felt one foot slip into empty space as he reached the edge of the walkway. He twisted his body, pulling himself away from the edge, trying to keep Tane in sight. He saw the merc's knife arcing around again, and threw up an arm to block the slash. The knife clanged against the barrel of Cade's rifle, jarring it from his tired fingers. He let it fall, concentrating on regaining his balance, ducking under the next cut of the knife, then launched himself at Tane. He slammed into the merc, hearing the man grunt.

Locked together, they crashed against the tunnel side, scraping flesh against the rough surface. Cade reached out and locked his fingers around Tane's wrist, pushing the keen edge of the knife away from his throat. He failed to stop Tane's knee as it drove up at his body and felt pain erupt across his ribs. He shoved hard, swinging Tane around, and head-butted the merc in the face. Something cracked, and Tane's nose gushed blood. The merc blinked away the tears of pain and slammed his knee into Cade's side again. The blow burst the edges of the bullet gouge in Cade's side, and he felt the soft pulse of warm blood coursing down his body.

Letting Tane pull him away from the tunnel's wall, Cade swung his free fist in a short, vicious jab that connected with his opponent's jaw. Cade repeated the blow a couple more times, drawing blood in the end.

In desperation, Tane jammed his arm across Cade's throat and shoved hard, trying to cut off his air supply and also bend his spine. For long seconds they shuffled back and forth across the walkway, coming close to the edge, then drawing away. Tane's foot slipped on the concrete, leaving him off guard as he tried to right himself.

Cade realized his moment was there. He rammed his right knee up into Tane's groin with every ounce of strength left in him. There was no holding back. The blow was delivered with total force and it hit with crippling intensity. Tane's howl filled the tunnel. The pain that erupted throughout his body left him completely helpless. Cade pulled down on Tane's knife arm, smashing the wrist across his knee, and the knife flew from Tane's grasp. Continuing his move, Cade caught hold of Tane's collar with his free hand, spun his own body in toward Tane, leaning forward and rolling the merc across his hip. With a pull on Tane's collar and the arm he still held, he threw the merc over his shoulder in a classic judo move.

Tane was tossed over the edge of the walkway. He fell, and a short scream rose from his throat that ceased abruptly as his back slammed down on the steel monorail. Tane's spine broke with an audible crack, and he was left dangling from the rail, his limbs trembling in a final spasm before death claimed him.

Cade pulled his handgun, looking around for Amos Sinclair. The industrialist was nowhere in sight. He had deserted Tane and continued on into the complex alone.

Following the walkway, Cade reached an open door. He stepped through and found himself in a long, softly lit corridor. The floor underfoot felt cushiony and seemed to move beneath his feet. The air was warm, and he could feel a gentle current coming from the overhead vents.

He moved along the corridor, following the natural curve in the smooth walls. Reaching an intersection, Cade caught sight of Sinclair. The industrialist was a long way ahead. He was moving swiftly, clearly in a hurry but not appearing to be in any panic. The man was still sure of himself, Cade decided. Despite everything, Sinclair would still be figuring he could manage to come out untouched. He was incapable of accepting defeat and would resist right up to the end.

Cade lifted his handgun and tracked the distant figure. He held his target for a moment, then lowered the gun. The distance was too great for him to be sure of his shot. He found a wry smile hovering on his lips. Janek would have made the shot without hesitation.

Sinclair had reached his destination. He paused at a wall panel and keyed in some numbers. A door slid open, and he vanished from sight. Cade broke into a run, trying to ignore the ugly burn of pain in his side. He touched a hand to his shirt and felt his fingers wet with blood.

He reached the door just before it glided closed. That was a mistake on Sinclair's part—not securing the door once he'd gone through. Maybe he wasn't as rational as Cade had imagined.

There was a flight of stairs ahead of Cade. He went up, moving sideways and keeping his back to the wall. At the top he found himself in another corridor and saw that the wall facing him was supplied with observation windows. Cade glanced through as he moved along the corridor. He found he was looking down into vast storage warehouses. They were lined with rows and rows of neatly parked machines of different shapes and sizes that seemed to go on forever.

Cade reached an elevator door. The light on the indicator panel was showing the levels the elevator was dropping to.

It stopped on sublevel 4.

Cade waited a couple of minutes then called the elevator back. He stepped in and punched in sublevel 4.

The elevator dropped like a stone. Cade leaned against the back wall of the car, breathing deeply and pressing his left hand over the bleeding gash in his side.

The descending car slowed and stopped with irritating accuracy. The doors slid open and Cade cautiously stepped out of the car.

He was in a storage area similar to the ones he'd seen above. Only this one didn't house rows of machines.

Stretching out in front of Cade were ranks of combat droids. Hundreds of them, identical to the ones Cade and Janek had faced during the past few days. The sight of the angular-featured, black-clad droids left Cade with a cold chill down his spine.

He realized he was looking at Amos Sinclair's last line of defense. The industrialist had kept these droids in reserve, banking on them doing the job for him if all else failed.

Cade turned as a faint sound reached him. He moved along the shadowed wall of the storage area, his gun tracking ahead of him. Easing around a wall extension, Cade saw a computer terminal and metal storage cabinets.

Amos Sinclair was immersed in some business at the computer. His attention was focused fully on the microchip panel he was inserting in the computer's port, and he failed to notice Cade's presence until a hand caught hold of his arm and yanked him away from the keyboard. He stumbled back but managed to regain his balance. He straightened and fixed Cade with a contemptuous and withering glance.

"Why, it's our upholder of law and order," Sinclair said derisively. "Haven't you done enough, Marshal Cade?"

"Not yet," Cade replied. "Isn't this a touch over the top even for a crazy like you?"

"Crazy? Only in your eyes, Cade. As far as I see it, I'm doing this country a favor."

"Correction," Cade said. "You were trying. But that's over now, you sorry bastard."

"I detect something of a personal vendetta here . . . something beyond professional zeal."

"I lost a good friend because of you. A damn good cop, too."

"One man's fate in the balance . . . against the fate of a whole nation?" Sinclair smiled. "Hardly worth the bother."

"I don't think George Takagi would have seen it that way."

"Takagi? Oh, of course. The meddling NYPD tech who decided to poke his nose in where he shouldn't have. He got what he deserved."

"Glad you feel that way, Sinclair. Makes me feel a lot easier."

"What are you babbling about, man?"

"You agree people should get what they deserve?"

"Yes . . . I . . ." Sinclair's eyes widened, his face paling as he saw the reasoning behind Cade's question. "You can't. You won't kill me just like that. Not me. I'm too important for this country—"

Sinclair's hand moved toward his jacket, but Cade beat him to it. One smooth squeeze started the weapon spitting, but he kept firing until the auto's slide locked back on an empty chamber and Amos Sinclair was lying dead and bloody on the floor.

"Not anymore," he said coldly, then dropped the empty magazine from the gun and slipped in a fresh one. He cocked the weapon and put it away.

Before he left the storage area Cade pulled the microchip panel from the computer port and ground it under his heel. He took a last look at the ranks of immobile combat droids, imagining the chaos they could have caused if Sinclair had unleashed them on an unsuspecting city.

The thought remained at the back of his mind as he returned to where he'd left Janek guarding the conspiracy's three political allies.

As the monorail car slowed, Cade was able to see armed figures crowding the concourse around the helipad. Police cruisers were converging on the area, and overhead the air was loud with helicopters and air cruisers looking for landing spots. Cade climbed out of the car and made his slow way across the concourse.

He searched for friendly faces. At this distance they all looked the same—armed cops wearing body armor, and KC-200 patrol droids mingling with their human counterparts. Red-and-blue lights pulsed unceasingly as the wail of sirens competed with the grumble of motors and the endless chatter of radios.

Cade pulled his badge and showed it to a KC patrol droid as it crossed to intercept him.

"Marshal Janek has been concerned about you," the KC said. "And Lieutenant Schuberg has been looking for you."

"Where is the lieutenant?"

The KC led Cade across to one of the NYPD choppers. Cade spotted Schuberg, dressed in a bulky jumpsuit and a patrolman's leather jacket, directing a group of armed officers. As the Justice cop neared the group, Schuberg happened to look his way.

"T.J.? You son of a bitch, am I glad to see you." Schuberg looked Cade up and down. "You look like hell. What happened? Your suspects give you a hard time?"

Cade nodded. "Something like that. Looks like you pulled off your end of the deal."

Schuberg grinned. "Wasn't easy, but once we moved and took out the men at the top, the rest of the guys were with us."

"I figure most of them didn't even know what was happening."

"And that was what pissed most of them off. That, and the fact that Chief Norris had gone over to the other side."

"Well, he's resigned," Cade said.

"I saw," Schuberg remarked. He moved alongside Cade, leading him across to one of the other NYPD choppers. "How about Sinclair?"

"Paid his dues," Cade said.

"Fair enough," Schuberg said. "So what now?"

"Stabilize the situation. Pull in all the suspects. Let the President know, and Washington will get the ball rolling. We'll be up to our necks in paperwork for weeks. But let the other agencies handle it."

"You mean now that we've done all the dirty work for them?"

Cade grinned. "That's why we're here, Milt. The unsung heroes of the streets."

"We picked up your three local politicians," Schuberg announced. "I guess they'll have a hard time getting a vote next time around."

"It *is* a long way back from the Mars penal colony."

They reached the chopper, and Schuberg opened the hatch.

"Got someone here who needs to talk to you. And mind, treat this young woman with respect. She really helped us bring down a few of those men."

Cade glanced up in time to see Kate smiling down at him. She jumped to the ground and grabbed him around the neck.

"Damn you, T. J. Cade, I didn't know if you were alive or dead."

She saw the blood soaking his side, and she paled, her glance flying to his so she could assess the severity of the injury.

"It's okay," he said. "Just a scratch."

"A scratch? You are bleeding all over the place."

Schuberg waved over a medic, but Cade had other things on his mind first.

"Hey, where's Janek?" he demanded.

"I'm here, Thomas," grumbled a familiar voice.

Cade turned and spotted the cyborg lying on a gurney.

"You off for a refit?" he asked, staring at the shredded wreckage of Janek's leg.

"We're flying him to Cybo Tech's facility in town," Schuberg said.

Cade grinned. "Any excuse so you can go flirt with Dr. Landers."

"That's not true," Janek snapped. "This has nothing to do with Abby . . . Dr. Landers."

No one said a word, leaving the cyborg staring back and forth between them, his mood darkening.

"This is a genuine emergency," Janek insisted.

"Sure, partner."

Janek scowled at him. "It is *my* leg," he said. "You have to realize, Thomas. I was very attached to it."

These heroes can't be beat!
Celebrate the American hero with this collection of never-before-published installments of America's finest action teams—ABLE TEAM, PHOENIX FORCE and VIETNAM: GROUND ZERO—only in Gold Eagle's

Available for the first time in print, eight new hard-hitting and complete episodes of America's favorite heroes are contained in three action-packed volumes:

In **HEROES: Book I**   July $5.99   592 pages

ABLE TEAM: Razorback by Dick Stivers
PHOENIX FORCE: Survival Run by Gar Wilson
VIETNAM: GROUND ZERO: Zebra Cube by Robert Baxter

In **HEROES: Book II**   August $5.99   592 pages

PHOENIX FORCE: Hell Quest by Gar Wilson
ABLE TEAM: Death Lash by Dick Stivers
PHOENIX FORCE: Dirty Mission by Gar Wilson

In **HEROES: Book III**   September $4.99   448 pages

ABLE TEAM: Secret Justice by Dick Stivers
PHOENIX FORCE: Terror in Warsaw by Gar Wilson

Celebrate the finest hour of the American hero with your copy of the Gold Eagle HEROES collection.

Available in retail stores in the coming months.   HEROES

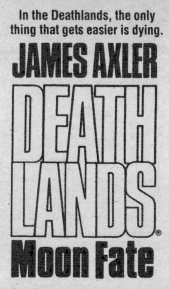